Marie stared at him

She'd thought that she and Alex had shared their secrets over the years, but he'd obviously been holding something back.

"So you're…a prince?"

He gave her a pained look. "Belkraine no longer exists as a separate country. I'm not sure how you can be a prince of something that doesn't exist."

He was missing the point. The role of many monarchies had changed in the last hundred years, but privilege and money was something that didn't change.

"A prince in exile, then."

"Strictly speaking a king…in exile."

"But—"

Marie bit her tongue.

Suddenly she couldn't bear it. The man she'd thought of as her friend, who she'd dared to kiss and loved every minute of it… Marie sprang from her seat, marching over to the window and staring out at the street. Maybe that would anchor her down, keep her feet firmly on the ground, and she could begin to address the question of whether this really was Alex anymore, or just a stranger who looked like him.

Dear Reader,

I've wanted to write a friends-to-lovers story for a long time. Friends who know everything about each other and manage to steer their way through the difficult waters of transforming their relationship into a romance. But I wondered what might happen if those friends find that they really don't know everything about each other...

When Marie Davies finds that she didn't even know her best friend's real name, she feels betrayed. Couldn't Alex have trusted her enough to tell her about his family's royal history, when he knows everything about her? In order to work together and make their professional dreams a reality, Alex and Marie must salvage their broken friendship. Understanding why Alex couldn't share his secret may remove the last barrier that stands between them, but can Marie ever really trust Alex enough to love him?

Thank you for reading Alex and Marie's story! I love to hear from readers, and you can contact me via my website at annieclaydon.co.uk

Annie x

BEST FRIEND TO ROYAL BRIDE

———

ANNIE CLAYDON

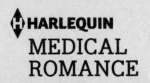

HARLEQUIN

MEDICAL
ROMANCE

HARLEQUIN®
MEDICAL
ROMANCE™

Recycling programs
for this product may
not exist in your area.

ISBN-13: 978-1-335-14921-3

Best Friend to Royal Bride

Copyright © 2020 by Annie Claydon

This edition published by arrangement with Harlequin Books S.A.

For questions and comments about the quality of this book,
please contact us at CustomerService@Harlequin.com.

Harlequin Enterprises ULC
22 Adelaide St. West, 40th Floor
Toronto, Ontario M5H 4E3, Canada
www.Harlequin.com

Printed in U.S.A.

Books by Annie Claydon

Harlequin Medical Romance

Pups that Make Miracles

Festive Fling with the Single Dad

London Heroes

Falling for Her Italian Billionaire
Second Chance with the Single Mom

Single Dad Docs

Resisting Her English Doc

Stranded in His Arms

Rescued by Dr. Rafe
Saved by the Single Dad

The Doctor She'd Never Forget
Discovering Dr. Riley
The Doctor's Diamond Proposal
English Rose for the Sicilian Doc
Saving Baby Amy
Forbidden Night with the Duke
Healed by the Single Dad Doc
From Doctor to Princess?
Firefighter's Christmas Baby

Visit the Author Profile page
at Harlequin.com for more titles.

CHAPTER ONE

The first Friday in February

THE EVENING OF the first Friday in February had been marked out as *'busy'* in Marie's calendar for the last twelve years. As she looked around the table, stacked with food and wine, twelve people all talking at once, she could only hope that it would be booked for the next twelve years.

During her final year at medical school there had been one class that was special. A tight-knit group who had laughed together and shared the ups and downs of their studies. Since then they'd graduated and gone their separate ways, but one evening every year still belonged to them.

Sunita was passing her phone around so that everyone could see the pictures of her new baby. Will was just back from America, and Rae had stories to tell about Africa. Nate was having relationship problems, and was talking intently to David, who was nodding thoughtfully. When she got the chance, Marie would change seats and offer what support she could.

And Alex...

Marie didn't like to admit it, but she looked forward to seeing him the most. He had been the golden boy of the class, managing to combine a carefree love of life and a wicked sense of fun with academic brilliance. He and Marie had struck up an especially close friendship and, in truth, if you were looking for anything long-term with Alex, then friendship was the way to go. He was seldom without a girlfriend, but those relationships never lasted very long.

Tonight he looked as if he had things on his mind. He'd flipped through Sunita's photographs, grinning and saying all the right things, but when he'd passed the phone on he'd gone back to playing with his food and staring abstractedly into space.

Marie leaned over, feeling the softness of his cashmere sweater as she brushed her fingers against his arm to get his attention. 'What's going on, Alex?'

'I'm…coasting at the moment. One hand on the driving wheel with the wind in my hair.' He shrugged, smiling suddenly. Those long-lashed grey eyes were still the same, and so was his mop of dark hair, shorter now but still as thick.

The memory was as fresh as if it had been yesterday. Alex pulling up outside her student digs, the soft top of his car pulled back, saying he just wanted to feel the warm breeze on his face and would Marie like to keep him company? It was a world away from the worries that seemed to be lingering behind his smile now.

'And you're still moving mountains?'

Marie laughed. 'I'm still shovelling, if that's what you mean.'

'Moving mountains one shovelful at a time. That's your speciality.'

He made it sound like a good thing. Something that was fine and virtuous, and not just a fact of life. Her life, anyway.

Alex had never had to worry about money, and had received a generous allowance from his family. Marie had gone to medical school knowing that her family needed her help rather than the other way around. Hand to mouth, taking each day as it came. Mostly she'd had enough to eat and cover her rent, but sometimes it had been a struggle. She'd made it through, one shovelful at a time.

On the other side of the restaurant a waiter was bringing a cake, flaming with candles, to a table of six young women. He started to sing 'Happy Birthday' and the tune was taken up around all the tables. Alex was watching, singing quietly, and Marie wondered whether he had any wishes tonight.

The birthday girl stood up, leaning over the cake. And suddenly Alex was moving, ducking adroitly past a couple of waiters and making his way towards her. It wasn't until Marie was on her feet that she saw what the matter was. The girl was waving her arm, which only fanned the flames licking at her sleeve.

Stop, drop and roll. She hadn't done the first, and it looked as if she wasn't going to do the second or the third either. Alex reached her just as she started to panic, grabbing her arm and deftly catching up a pitcher of water from the table.

Suddenly the restaurant was deathly quiet, the girl's keening sobs the only sound. Alex had his arm tightly around her and he flashed Marie a glance, to check that she would stay with the other young women at the table, before hurrying their injured friend towards the ladies' restroom.

'Where are they going? We'll go with her...'

One of the party rose from her seat and Marie motioned to her to sit down again. She knew Alex had this under control, and if he'd needed any help he would have left no one in any doubt about what he wanted them to do.

'It's okay, we're doctors. The burn should be cooled straight away and that's what my colleague has gone to do. It's best that we stay here.'

Alex would be checking for signs of shock, and being surrounded by people wasn't going to help.

'But...is she going to be all right? She was on fire...' Another of the friends spoke up.

Things could have been a lot worse. It had looked as if her blouse was cotton, not a man-made fabric, and the flames had spread relatively slowly. If Alex hadn't acted so quickly precious minutes would have been lost...

'The fire was extinguished very quickly. I'll go and check on her.'

Marie turned towards her own table, where everyone was watchful but still in their seats, trusting that Marie or Alex would call them if they were needed. She beckoned to Sunita, who rose from her seat, weaving her way past the tables towards them, and asked her to stay with the group of friends.

A waiter was standing outside the restroom and let Marie through. Inside, Alex had sat the young woman by a basin and was gently supporting her arm under a stream of lukewarm water. He was smiling, his voice gentle and relaxed as he chatted to her quietly.

'How many candles on that cake, Laura?'

'Eighteen. It's my eighteenth birthday tomorrow. I'm having a party.' Laura turned the corners of her mouth down.

'You'll be fine. This is a first-degree burn, which is the least severe. It's going to hurt for a little while, but it won't leave a scar. You're going to have a great birthday.' He glanced up at Marie. 'This is my friend, Marie. She's a doctor too, so she can't help poking her nose in and making sure I'm doing everything right.'

Alex shot her a delicious smile, the kind that reminded Marie of when they'd been young doctors together in A&E. Laura turned towards Marie, and Alex steadied her arm under the water.

'He's doing pretty well.'

'Glad to hear it. What about you? How are you doing?'

'I'm all right. Where is everyone? Are they eating my cake?'

'They sent me to find out how you were. They're not eating the cake.'

Alex had done a great job of keeping Laura calm if her main concern was cake.

'That's a relief,' Alex broke in. 'Laura's promised me a slice. Not for another ten minutes, though. We need to keep cooling the burn. Then I think we'll send you off home, with a list of instructions.'

'Oh, you're going to write a list of *instructions*?' Marie grinned conspiratorially at Laura. 'Watch out for those.'

Alex chuckled. 'First on the list is to have a very happy birthday…'

Things might have been so different. Laura's eighteenth birthday could have been spent in a burns unit, with a prognosis of skin grafts and a great deal of pain. But she was going home with her friends, a little wet from the pitcher of water that Alex had poured on her arm to extinguish the flames, and with a couple of miraculously minor burns. Whatever future she wanted for herself was still waiting for her.

Alex spent another half an hour making sure she was all right, and advising her on how to care for the burns. Sunita had persuaded Laura's friends to come over and sit with her, and the cake was being divided into portions and wrapped. The low hum of chatter in the restaurant indicated that the incident was already largely forgotten, cleared away along with the debris from Laura's table.

Alex had gone outside to see Laura and her friends into a taxi, and Marie saw him turn, leaning back against the railings that separated the pavement from the front of the restaurant, staring up at the scrap of sky that showed between the tops of the buildings. It appeared that his easy, relaxed air had been all for Laura's sake.

Whatever the last year of medical school had thrown at them, Alex had always bounced back, but now he seemed brooding, almost heartbroken. There was definitely something wrong.

Maybe she could help. Maybe he'd stayed outside hoping she'd join him. It wouldn't be the first time they'd confided in each other, and Marie had always wanted him to feel he could talk to her about anything.

She picked up Alex's jacket from the back of his chair and slipped away from the table.

Alex had been looking forward to seeing Marie again. He'd wondered whether he should confide in her, and now that he'd sent Laura safely on her way the yearning to do so reasserted itself. He knew he wouldn't, though. Marie normally understood everything, but she wouldn't be able to understand how difficult the last few months had been. She'd struggled for everything she had, and it felt somehow wrong to confide his pain and dismay at finding he had much more than enough of everything.

'Aren't you cold?'

When he heard her voice it didn't come as much of a surprise. Maybe that was what he was doing out here, shivering under the street lamps: waiting for Marie to come and find him.

'Not really.' He took his jacket from her, wrapping it around her shoulders. The pleasure he got from the gesture seemed way out of proportion to its true worth.

'That was a bit like old times.'

She turned her gaze on him and suddenly it felt a lot like old times.

'Yes. I'm glad Laura's okay.'

'She has you to thank for that. So, since we seem to be out here, and your jacket's nice and warm...' Marie gave him an impish smile. 'You can tell me what the matter is.'

It was tempting. Alex had never been able to resist her eyes. Almost violet in the sunlight and deep blue in the shade. She wore her dark hair in a shining pixie cut, and Alex always thought of mischief and magic when he looked at her.

'I'm fine...just tired. You remember tired?' He smiled at her.

She chuckled. 'Remember that time you came round to my place and I'd been up all night working on abstracts?'

'I've never seen anyone actually fall asleep *while* they're drinking coffee before. Particularly since I'd made it so strong...'

Marie had got a job writing abstracts for scientific papers, which had been more lucrative than waitressing and had fitted around their busy study schedule better. Working and studying at the same time had been a struggle for her, but Alex had learned early in their friendship that she never took help from anyone.

Suddenly he was back in that time when he'd first felt completely free. Marie's two shabby rooms, right at the top of a multiple-occupancy house, had been as clean as one pair of hands could scrub them, and full of outrageous low-cost colour.

'Funny thing about that...' Marie gave him a knowing look. 'When I woke up you were gone, but I sat down to review my abstracts and found they were all perfect. Not a spelling or grammar mistake in any of them.'

Alex had reckoned he'd got away with that. He'd tried to make Marie stand up but she'd slumped against him, still asleep, so he'd had to practically carry her into the bedroom. He'd taken off her cardigan and shoes and decided to stop there, covering her up with the brightly patterned quilt. He'd sometimes imagined their two bodies naked together under that quilt. But Marie was far too good a friend, too good a person, to contemplate having a throwaway romance with her.

Alex had glanced at the document that was open on her laptop, meaning to close it down. He'd seen a mistake in the text, and had sat down and worked through everything, correcting the slips that fatigue had forced upon her.

'You must do your best work when you're flying on autopilot.' He tried to maintain a straight face.

'I suppose I must. Apparently I also spell synthesise with a *z*.'

'Really? There must be a study in there somewhere. How fatigue alters your spelling choices.' Alex shrugged guiltily. 'They're both correct, according the dictionary.'

'Yes, they are. Although I imagine that "ize" as a verb ending is considered either an anachronism or an American spelling these days.' She smirked at him.

'You can mock if you want. Just because I went to a school that prided itself on having been the same for the last few hundred years…' Alex had hated school. It had been only slightly less snobby and suffocating than his parents' home.

'I'm not mocking; I thought it was very sweet of you.' She took a step towards him. 'Along with all those expensive textbooks you used to lend me. And dropping round to pick me up so I didn't have to take the bus.'

'Why bring that up all of a sudden? Just to let me know I'm not as tactful as I thought I was?' Alex wondered if he was in for a lecture about how she could have managed perfectly well on her own.

Marie shook her head. 'You were *very* tactful. I hardly even noticed what you were doing most of the time. And you were my friend and you helped me. That's something that goes both ways.'

He knew that. But he couldn't talk to Marie about this. 'I'm fine. Really. And I appreciate your concern.'

'Just as long as you know that I'm always here for you.'

She reached out, touching his arm, and Alex almost flinched. All his senses were crying out for comfort, and yet he just couldn't bring himself to ask. Was this the way she'd felt, despite all her self-sufficiency?

'I know. Thank you.'

He'd meant to give her a basic friendly hug, the kind he'd given her so many times before. But when he felt her body against his he couldn't let her go. Marie seemed to be the one thing in his life that wasn't tainted right now.

He leaned down to kiss her cheek. But she turned her head and his lips brushed hers. Before he could tear himself away her gaze met his, her eyes midnight-blue in the darkness.

What if…?

What if…?

What if he could turn his back on the vision of his parents' unhappy marriage and sustain a relationship for more than a few months? What if he could trust himself to get involved with the one person he cared about the most, even knowing he might break her heart and his? And what if everything he'd sought to escape hadn't just caught him again in its iron clutches?

They were all serious questions that needed to be asked and answered before he took the step of kissing her. But then he felt her lips touch his and he was lost. Or maybe this was exactly what it was like to find himself. Alex wasn't sure.

She was soft and sweet, and when he kissed her again she responded. Maybe it lasted a moment and maybe an hour. All Alex knew was that it was impossible to attach a time frame to something that was complete and perfect.

Even the way she drew away from him was perfect. A little sigh of regret, her eyes masked by her eyelashes.

He'd always supposed that kissing Marie was the one thing he mustn't do. The one thing he wouldn't be able to come back from. But in a sudden moment of clarity he realised that kissing her had only made him more determined that he couldn't do it. Marie wasn't just another pretty face he could walk away from without looking back. She was his friend, and he wanted her for a lifetime, not just a few months.

'Do you want to go back in?' If it meant keeping her then he had to let her go.

She still wouldn't look at him. 'Yes…'

He felt her move in his arms and let her go. Marie looked up at him for a moment, and he almost forgot that this had been a very bad idea that had the power to spoil something that had been good for years. Then suddenly she was gone, back into the restaurant to take her seat at the table again.

Alex waited, knowing the group always swapped places between courses, so everyone got to speak to everyone else. When he went back inside there was a free seat for him at the other end of the table from Marie. Alex sat down without looking at her, and was immediately involved in the heated debate about football which was going on between Emily and Will.

She didn't meet his gaze until the restaurant closed and a waitress pointedly fetched everyone's coats. Then, suddenly, he found himself standing next to her. He automatically helped her on with her coat and Marie smiled up at him.

'I'll see you next year. Be well, Alex.'

'Yes. Next year…'

He'd scarcely got the words out before she was gone. Marie had made her meaning clear. They were friends, and nothing was going to spoil that. Not fire, nor flood, nor even an amazing, heartshaking kiss. By next year it would be forgotten, and he and Marie would continue the way they always had.

The thought that he wouldn't see her again until next February seemed more heart-rending than any of the other challenges he'd faced in the last six months.

CHAPTER TWO

The first Friday in May

IT WAS ONLY four stops on the Tube from the central London hospital where Marie worked, but shining architecture and trendy bars had given way to high-rise flats, corner shops and families with every kind of problem imaginable.

Marie knew about some of those problems first-hand. She'd grown up fifteen minutes' walk away from the address that Alex had given her. Her father had left when she was ten, and her mother had retreated into a world of her own. Four miserable months in foster care had seen Marie separated from her three younger brothers, and when the family had got back together again she'd resolved that she'd keep it that way.

It had cost Marie her childhood. Looking after her brothers while her mother had worked long hours to keep them afloat financially. She'd learned how to shop and cook, and at the weekends she'd helped out by taking her brothers to the park, reading her schoolbooks while they played.

It had been hard. And lonely. After she'd left home she'd had a few relationships, but knowing exactly what it meant to be abandoned had made her cautious. She'd never found the kind of love that struck like a bolt of lightning, dispelling all doubts and fears, and the continuing need to look after her family didn't give her too much time for regrets.

When she reached the Victorian building it looked just as ominous as she remembered it, its bricks stained with grime and three floors towering above her like a dark shadow in the evening sunshine. The high cast-iron gates creaked as Marie pulled them open, leaving flakes of paint on her hands.

'This had better not be a joke…'

It wasn't a joke. Alex's practical jokes were usually a lot more imaginative than this. And when he'd called her it had sounded important. He'd made a coded reference to their kiss, saying that he wanted her to come as a professional favour to a friend, which told Marie that he'd done exactly as she'd hoped and moved past it. That was both a relief and a disappointment.

She pushed the thought of his touch to the back of her mind and made her way across the cracked asphalt in front of the building. There was a notice taped to the main door that advertised that this was the 'Living Well Clinic'. Marie made a face at the incongruous nature of the name and pressed the buzzer, wondering if it was going to work.

The door creaked open almost immediately.

'Hi. Thanks so much for coming.' Alex was looking unusually tense.

'My pleasure. What's all this about, Alex?'

'Come and see.' He stood back from the doorway and Marie stepped inside, trying not to flinch as the door banged shut behind them.

'Oh! This is a bit different from how I remember it.'

At the other end of the small lobby was an arch, which had been sandblasted back to the original brick, its colour and texture contrasting with the two glass doors that now filled the arch. As Marie approached them they swished back, allowing her into a large bright reception space, which had once been dingy cloakrooms.

And it wasn't finished yet. Cabling hung from the ceiling and the walls had obviously been re-plastered recently, with dark spots showing where they were still drying out. One of the curved-top windows had been replaced, and the many layers of paint on the others had been sanded back, leaving the space ready for new decoration.

'You know this place?'

'Yes, I went to school here.'

'Did you?' He grinned awkwardly. 'I wish

I'd known. I would have looked for your name carved on one of the desks.'

'You wouldn't have found it.'

'Too busy studying?'

'Something like that.'

Leaving her name in this place might have signified that she would look back on her schooldays with a measure of nostalgia, when they'd been no more than a means to an end. They'd been something she'd had to do so she could move on and leave them behind. Just like she'd left that kiss behind. The one she couldn't stop thinking about…

'What's going on, Alex? Are you working here now or is this something you're involved with in your spare time?'

'I don't have spare time any more. I'm here full-time; I gave up working with the practice.'

Alex had always said he'd do something like this, and now he'd actually done it. The next logical step from his job as a GP in a leafy London suburb would have been to go into private practice, and Alex had the contacts and the reputation to make the transition easy. But he'd given all that up to come and work here, in a community where his expertise was most sorely needed.

'And you'll be seeing patients here?'

'As soon as we don't have to supply them with hard hats.' He bent, picking up two safety helmets and handing her one. 'Come and see what's been going on.'

As he showed her around, the scale of the project became obvious. Some of the classrooms had been divided into two to make treatment rooms, with high ceilings and plenty of light from the arched windows. A state-of-the-art exercise suite was planned for the ground floor, which would be staffed by physiotherapists and personal trainers, and the old school hall was being converted into a coffee shop and communal area. Upstairs there was provision for dieticians and other health advisors, along with a counselling suite and rooms for self-help groups of all kinds.

'We'll have facilities for DEXA scanning in here...' He opened the door of one of the old science labs, which had now been reduced to a shell. 'Along with other diagnostic equipment. There's a space for the mobile breast-screening unit to park at the side of the building, and when the clinic's finished it'll be part of its regular route. We'll be able to undertake general health screening as well.'

'It's wonderful, Alex. Everything under one roof.'

The project was ambitious and imaginative, and would be of huge benefit to the local community.

'That's the idea. It's a kind of one-stop shop,

and although it'll cater for complex medical needs it's also going to be for people who just want a healthier lifestyle.'

'What's going to happen with the courtyards?'

They were walking along a corridor that looked out onto one of the two central light wells. They were one of the few things that remained unchanged, and the dingy concrete floors were a reminder of what this place had once been like.

Alex shrugged. 'There are no plans for them just yet. Some planting might be nice.'

'And what about the old gym?' The annexe at the back of the school was enormous, and it seemed a waste not to use it for something.

'We made a discovery. Come and see.'

He led the way to the large double doors that opened onto the gym and Marie gasped. The folding seats had been taken out and light from windows on three sides flooded into the space. Instead of sprung wooden floors there was a large concrete-sided hole.

'That's not...not a swimming pool, is it?'

He nodded. 'When we looked at the plans we found that this annexe was built in the nineteen-thirties as a full-sized swimming pool. Later on it was made into a gym, but when we took up the floors we found that the pool had just been filled in with hardcore and the foundations were still there and solid enough to use. There's room for a hydrotherapy pool, as well as the main pool.'

Alex seemed less excited about this than he should be. Maybe he was about to tell her that they'd run out of money, or had found some catastrophic problem with the building's structure and it was all about to fall down.

'This is marvellous. Are the pool and gym just for patients or are they available to the whole community?'

'There'll be a nominal charge, well below the usual rates. Anyone who's referred by a doctor or one of the medical staff here won't have to pay anything.' Alex was suddenly still, looking at her thoughtfully. 'What about you? Would you be interested in being part of it all?'

That sounded a bit like the stuff that fairy tales were made of. A gloomy old castle brought to life and transformed. Alex would fit in there quite nicely as the handsome Prince. But something about the quiet certainty in his manner stopped Marie from brushing the suggestion off.

'You'd put in a good word with the boss for me?'

'It's more a matter of putting a good word in with you. We'd be lucky to get you.'

Excitement trickled down Marie's spine. This was real. In that case, Marie needed to ask a few real questions.

'What exactly is your role here, Alex?'

He frowned, as if that might be a problem. 'It's rather a long story… Why don't you come to my office and we'll have some coffee?'

Marie followed him to a small suite of offices situated at the front of the building, off the main reception area. From here it would be possible to see all the comings and goings, and Marie guessed that Alex would have had a hand in the location of his office. He always liked to be in the thick of things.

His office was one of the few rooms in the building that was finished, but it didn't seem much like the kind of place the Alex she remembered would like. The cream walls and tall windows lent themselves to minimalism, but Alex didn't.

'How long have you been here, Alex?'

'A couple of months.' He looked around at the sleek wooden desk that stood at one end of the room and the comfortable easy chairs grouped around a coffee table at the other end. 'Why?'

Alex had been here for two months? And he hadn't yet covered the walls with pictures and stamped his own personality on the space? That wasn't like him at all. Perhaps the clinic had some kind of rule about that.

'It just seems a bit…unlived-in.' Marie looked around for something, anything, to comment on, instead of asking whether all that light and clear space hurt his eyes. She nodded towards the stylish chair behind his desk. 'I like your chair.'

'I reckoned I'd be sitting in it for enough hours, so I wanted something that was comfortable. Give it a try.'

He walked over to the wood-framed cupboards that lined one wall, opening one of the doors to reveal a coffee machine and a small sink unit.

The chair was great—comfortable and supportive—and when Marie leaned back the backrest tipped gently with her movement. She started to work her way around all the levers and knobs under the seat.

'I love this. It's got more controls than my first car.'

She got to her feet as Alex brought the coffee and he motioned her to sit again, smiling as if it hurt his face to do so.

'You've missed a few of the adjustments. The knob on the left lets you tip the seat forward.' He sat down in one of the chairs on the other side of the desk.

'Oh!' Marie tried it, almost skinning her knuckles on the stiff lever. 'Nice one. I'm glad to see the clinic practises what it preaches and looks after its staff.'

She was just talking. Saying things that might fill the space between them and hoping to provoke a reaction. She'd never seen Alex look so worried before.

Not worried…

Burdened.

It was time to grasp the nettle and find out what was going on. She leaned forward, putting her elbows on the desk as if she were about to interview him. 'So what's the story then, Alex? I'm intrigued, so start right at the beginning.'

He paused, staring into his mug, as if that would tell him exactly where the beginning was.

'A hundred and ten years ago…'

'What? Really?'

He gave her a strained smile and Marie regretted the interruption. Whatever had happened a hundred and ten years ago must be more important than it sounded.

'You said start at the beginning.'

'I did. Sorry…' She waved him on and there was silence for a moment. Then he spoke again.

'A hundred and ten years ago the King of Belkraine was deposed and his family fled to London. They brought with them a lot of very valuable jewels, the title deeds to property in this country, and what was literally a king's ransom in investments. His eldest son was my grandfather.'

Marie stared at him.

She'd thought that she and Alex had shared most of their secrets over the years but he'd obviously been holding back. Marie wasn't entirely sure how she felt about that.

'So you're...a prince?'

He gave her a pained look. 'Belkraine no longer exists as a separate country. I'm not sure how you can be a prince of something that doesn't exist.'

He was missing the point. The role of many monarchies had changed in the last hundred years, but privilege and money was something that didn't change.

'A prince in exile, then?'

'Strictly speaking a king...in exile. My father died in June last year.'

'Alex, I'm so sorry.'

'Thank you. But it's... We'd been estranged for some years. Ever since I first went to medical school.'

'But—'

Marie bit her tongue. He'd never spoken much about his family, but she knew that he was an only child and that his parents lived in a big house in the country somewhere. There hadn't ever been any mention of an estrangement, and Marie had always assumed he came from a normal happy family.

Now wasn't the time to mention that this was what Alex had allowed everyone to believe. He had no chance to make things right with his father now.

'That must have hurt you a great deal.'

He shrugged. 'That door closed a long time ago. I came to terms with it.'

There were too many questions, piling up on top of each other like grains of sand in an hourglass. What was Alex doing here? Why had he never said anything about this before?

Maybe she should just stay silent and listen.

Alex glanced at her uncertainly and Marie motioned for him to keep talking.

'I didn't expect that my father would leave me anything, let alone his whole estate. But he did. I find that I have more money than I know what to do with.'

'How much…?'

It wasn't good manners to ask, but money had never bothered Alex all that much. If this was a life-changing amount, then that was both good news and bad. Good, because he could do the things he'd always wanted to. Bad, because he seemed so burdened by it.

'If you include all the assets and property then it runs into something more than two billion. Less than three.'

She stared at him. That was the kind of number that Marie would never get her head around, so it was probably better not to even try.

'And this… *You've* done all this?' She waved her finger in a wild circle.

'My ancestors viewed wealth as a way to gain power and more wealth. I want to spend the money a little more wisely than that.'

It was worthy. Altruistic. Right now it was about all she recognised of the Alex that she knew. The smiling, carefree soul who was in the habit of taking one day at a time had gone.

'Wait a minute…' A thought struck her. Had Alex been hiding all this in plain sight? 'Alex *King*?'

'Dr Alex King is who I really am. But my birth certificate says Rudolf Aloysius Alexander König.'

Suddenly she couldn't bear it. She hadn't even known his *name*? The man she'd thought of as her friend, whom she'd dared to kiss and had loved every minute of it…

Marie sprang from her seat, marching over to the window and staring out at the street. Maybe that would anchor her down, keep her feet firmly on the ground, and then she could begin to address the question of whether this really was Alex any more, or just a stranger who looked like him.

Marie wasn't taking this well. It was almost a relief. The small number of other people he'd had to tell about this had congratulated him on his sudden and immense wealth and started to treat him as if he was suddenly something different. It was typical of Marie that her objection to the whole thing wasn't what he'd expected. She brushed aside the money and his royal status as if they didn't exist. All she cared about was that she hadn't known his name.

'King is a translation of König. Alex is my middle name...' He ventured an explanation.

She shook her head. 'I thought I knew you, Alex...'

There was no point in telling her that a lot of people changed their names, or that a lot of people came from unhappy families. Marie was hurt that he'd never told her about any of it before. Maybe if she'd known his father she would have understood a little better.

'Rudolf König was the name my father gave to me to remind everyone who my family was. I wanted to make my own way in life, Marie, and to be measured by what *I've* done.'

'Yeah. I see that.' She was staring fixedly out of the window and didn't turn to face him.

'Then...?'

'Give me a minute. I'm processing.'

Okay. Processing didn't sound so terrible. If Marie could come to any conclusions then he'd like to hear them, because all he'd felt since he'd heard about his father's will was that he was being dragged back into a life from which he'd previously torn himself. Money and status had soured his parents' lives, and it already felt like it was slowly squeezing all the joy out of his.

She turned slowly, leaning back against the windowsill and regarding him thoughtfully.

'So…it's still Alex, is it?' Not *Your Majesty...*?'

'You don't need to rub it in, Marie. Who the hell else do you think I know how to be?'

Her face softened and she almost smiled. It was one step towards the warmth that he craved.

'Sorry.' She pressed her lips together in thought. 'Who knows about this?'

'A few people that I know from school. No one here. But it's not a secret. I just don't talk about it.'

She turned to face him, her eyes full of violet fire. 'Isn't that what secrets are? Things you keep from your friends?'

'I *never* lied.' He heard himself snap, and took a breath. 'I want the clinic to be about the work and not about me.'

'It *is* about you, though. You built it.'

'I facilitated it. I want people to talk about the things we do here, and talking about who I am is only going to divert attention away from that.'

Alex decided to leave aside the fact that he really didn't want to talk about who he was, because that would be a matter of reopening old wounds.

Marie was nodding slowly. It was time to take a risk.

'If you're not interested in a job here you can always just walk away.'

She pursed her lips. 'I never said I wasn't interested.'

Good. That was a start. He knew she'd seen the possibilities that the clinic offered, and maybe it was a matter of getting her to look at those and not at him. Not at the friend who'd broken the rules and kissed her. The friend who'd never told her about where he came from.

'This is the deal, then. This clinic is a flagship development, which is funded and run entirely by a trust I've set up with part of my inheritance. I don't want it to be the only one of its kind; it's intended that what we do here will be a model for future clinics all over the country. In order to achieve that we'll need to attract extra funding from outside sources.'

'You always did think big, Alex.'

He saw a flicker of excitement in her eyes. That was exactly the way *he* wanted to feel.

'I want you to share that vision with me as my co-director for the whole project. This clinic and future developments as well. You'll be able to dictate policy and do things on your own terms.'

She stared at him. 'Me? You want *me* to do that?'

Marie hadn't said no yet. He resisted the impulse to laugh and tell her that she could do anything she set her mind to doing. He was offering her the job on purely business grounds and he had to treat this conversation in that light.

'Your professional experience in A&E and diagnostic wards makes you ideally suited to the work here, where we're suggesting effective therapies and ways forward for patients. And you're not afraid of a challenge.' Alex allowed himself the smallest of smiles. 'That's one thing I happen to know about you.'

'This would be the first time I've taken on a management role.' Marie gave a little frown, obviously annoyed that she'd betrayed a little too much interest. 'If I decide to take the job, that is.'

'We already have a practice manager on board. She's very experienced and can advise on the practical aspects. It's your vision that matters, and your knowledge of what this community needs.'

'Is that your way of saying that you don't understand "poor people" and I do?'

She crooked two fingers to indicate quotation marks. There was a touch of defiance in her tone, and it would be very easy for Alex to say that the thought had never occurred to him.

'I think you understand some of the issues that people who live in this neighbourhood face. I want to formulate policies that are appropriate and which are going to work. If you want to boil that down to understanding poor people then be my guest.'

She grinned. He hadn't given her the expected answer, but it had been the right one.

'I think I *could* help…'

'I don't want you to *help*. This is a full partnership and I expect you to tell me what's wrong with my thinking.' He could trust Marie to do that. Their friendship was founded on it.

'It's a big step for me, Alex. I need to think about it.'

'Of course. Take as long as you like.'

Alex knew that Marie wouldn't take too long; she was nothing if not decisive. If she said no then that would be the end of it. But if she said yes then maybe, just maybe, she'd save him from being the man his father had wanted him to be and make him into the one *he* wanted to be.

By the time she got home Alex's email was already in her inbox, with a full job description and a detailed brief of his plans for the clinic appended. It took a while to read through it all, and Marie didn't finish until the early hours. She decided to sleep on it.

But sleeping on it didn't help, and neither did extending her usual running route around the park to almost twice the distance. Neither did staring at the wall or surfing the internet.

She wanted the job—very badly. It would give her a chance to shape policy and to be part of a bold initiative that promised to be a real force in helping people to live fuller and better lives.

But Alex...

Before she'd kissed him, before she'd known that he wasn't who he'd said he was...

That wasn't entirely fair. Thinking back, he'd never actually said anything about who he was. If it hadn't occurred to her to ask if his father was an immeasurably rich king in exile then maybe that was a lapse in imagination on her part.

But it still felt as if she'd kissed a man she didn't really know at all and had let herself fall a little in love with him. A future working closely with Alex seemed fraught with the dangerous unknown.

By Sunday evening she'd distilled it all down. There was no doubt in her mind that this was her dream job, but there were three things she wanted to know from Alex. Could he forget the kiss? Why hadn't he told her who he was? And what did the clinic really mean to him?

They were tricky questions. She had to find a way of asking indirectly, and after an hour of scribbling and crossing out she had three questions that might or might not elicit the information she wanted.

Marie picked up her phone and typed a text.

Are you still awake? I have some questions.

Nothing. Maybe he'd taken the evening off and gone out somewhere. Or maybe he was asleep already. As Marie put her phone down on the bed beside her, it rang.

'Hi, Alex…' She panicked suddenly and her mind went blank.

'Hi. Fire away, then.'

She'd rather hoped that she might ask by text, as that would give her a chance to carefully edit what she intended to say.

'Um…okay. Have you interviewed anyone else for this post?' That was the closest she could get to asking about the kiss.

'Nope.'

Marie rolled her eyes. 'That's not much help, so I'm going for a supplementary question. Why not?'

He chuckled 'You're asking if I offered you the job because we're friends? The answer's no. I need people around me who I trust and who are the best at what they do. If I wanted to meet up with you I'd call and ask if you were free for lunch.'

Okay. That sounded promising. Alex had drawn the line between professional and personal, and if he could take the kiss out of the equation then so could she.

'Next?'

Marie squeezed her eyes closed and recited the next question. 'That Christmas, at medical school, when we all went home for the holidays, what did you do?'

He was silent for so long that Marie began to wonder whether he'd hung up on her. She wondered if he knew how much this mattered, and why.

'Okay. I'll play. I stayed in my flat and watched TV all day.'

Marie caught her breath. He knew, and he'd answered honestly. 'You could have come to ours. You just had to say you were on your own.'

'You're *really* going to take that route, Marie? You'd have been too proud to let me bring as much as a box of mince pies with me. And you're wondering why I was too proud to admit that I was going to be on my own?'

Marie could understand that, even if she was sorry that he'd felt that way.

'Next question. And tell me you're not going to let me down by making this an easy one.'

Marie felt her ears start to burn. But that was Alex all over. He could be confrontational, but there was always that note of self-deprecatory laughter in his tone that made it all right.

'Do you think the clinic's going to save you, Alex?'

He was silent for a moment.

'Nice one. Those aren't the words I'd have used... But the inheritance is a responsibility, and I know from bitter experience that it's the kind of thing that can subsume a person. I want to hold on to who I am. So, yes, I guess I am hoping that the clinic will save me.'

These were the answers she'd wanted. And there was only one thing more to say.

'It's a great project, Alex. And, yes, I'd really like to take the job.'

CHAPTER THREE

THE MONTH'S NOTICE Marie had given at her old job had seemed like an age. She'd received daily email updates about what was going on at the clinic, and she'd spent many evenings and most of her weekends replying to Alex. If their exchanges seemed more businesslike than friendly, then that was all good. They needed to start as they meant to go on, and Marie was ready to begin work in earnest.

She knew what had been done, but that didn't match the effect of seeing it for herself. The facade of the building had been cleaned, exposing the soft yellow of the brick and the red terracotta detailing around the windows and door. The railings had been sanded and painted, and the old Tarmac playground was now a paved area, dotted with saplings that would soften the space as they grew. The main door had been stripped and varnished, and the dents from being kicked a thousand times as pupils had passed this way only added to its character.

The bell was new as well, and when she pressed it Alex appeared at the door, looking far less formal than his emails had been, and suspiciously like the man she'd dared to kiss. Maybe seeing him every day would quash that reaction.

Marie smiled nervously as he led her through the glass lobby doors. 'This is amazing!'

Everything was neat and tidy, with cream-painted walls and comfortable seating. Marie knew that the large curved barrier between the receptionist and the public space had been designed to protect the staff by stopping anyone from climbing across, but the sloping front looked like a thing of beauty and not a defence mechanism.

'I'm pleased with the way it's turned out.' Alex looked around as if this was the first time he'd seen the space. 'You didn't have to start until Monday, you know. How was your leaving party last night?'

Marie rolled her eyes. 'Long. We had too much cake, and then we went to the pub. I cried. I need something to do today to work off all the calories and the emotion.'

'You're not regretting this, are you?' He frowned.

'No. Looking forward to what's next doesn't mean I can't miss my old job a bit as well.'

He quirked his lips down, as if missing the past was something he'd been struggling with, and then smiled suddenly in an indication that he wasn't about to dwell on that.

'You want to see your new office?'

'Yes, please.'

Alex had suggested that she take the office next to his, but Marie wanted to be close to the two practice nurses and the health visitor who comprised their medical support team, and who would be located on the first floor. The problem had been solved by giving her an office that was directly above his and connected by a narrow private staircase.

'What do you think?'

Cream walls, lots of light and plenty of space. That was standard issue here, but no doubt she could inject a little colour of her own. Marie had chosen a light-framed wooden desk, and behind it was an identical chair to Alex's.

'You got me one of these!' Marie had wanted one, but hadn't wanted to ask.

'Yes. Call it an investment. I don't want you taking any time off sick with a bad back.'

Marie grinned at him and sat down, feeling the chair respond to her weight. 'I'll just take two days off to adjust it, shall I?'

'Mine took a week. The instructions are in your top drawer. Would you like to offer me some coffee?'

'Have I got any?'

Actually, Marie could do with some coffee.

The combination of cake and beer last night had left her feeling a little fuzzy this morning.

'Behind you.'

He indicated a door at the far end of the cupboards that lined one wall, and sat down in one of the chairs on the other side of the desk. Marie went to look and found that the door concealed a neat worktop with a coffee machine and supplies. A splash of colour next to the line of cream mugs caught her eye.

'You got me a mug!' She took the bright pink mug down from the shelf and examined it. 'With a flying pig! You remembered!'

'You always used to say that you wanted an office with a sofa, and time to sit and talk with your patients.'

The informal seating area in his office contained four easy chairs, covered in a chocolate-coloured fabric, but for Marie he had chosen a sofa and two chairs in a lighter cappuccino colour.

'And when you said that nothing was impossible, I told you that pigs might fly...' It had been a joke between them. 'Thank you, Alex.'

He seemed pleased with her reaction, but there was still a hint of reticence about his manner. The man Marie knew would have seen only exciting new opportunities, but Alex seemed burdened by his responsibilities.

He'd come round. The clinic would be opening next week, and as soon as it started to fill with people he'd respond to that. He was going to have to if this place was to reach its full potential. Alex had so much more than money to give, and it needed his creative enthusiasm to thrive.

Marie switched on the coffee machine, running her finger along the selection of different capsules. 'I'm going to have to try all of these, you know. I'll work from left to right.'

'I'd expect nothing less of you.'

When she put his cup down in front of him, he nodded a thank-you and pushed a manila envelope towards her. Marie opened it, tipping the contents out onto her desk.

'These are yours. The credit card is for any purchases you need to make, and the key card opens every door inside the clinic. Those two keys are for the main door, and the other one is the main override for the alarm system. The car keys are for the practice's vehicles.'

Marie laid the keys and cards out in front of her on the desk. This was the start of it all…

'The IT guy will be coming in on Monday to set up your computer. Let me know if there's anything else you need.' Alex got to his feet, picking up his mug. 'I'll leave you to settle in, if that's okay. I have a few things to do.'

Marie had wanted to share all this. Unpacking

the bag she'd brought with her and taking a tour of the clinic to see all the work that she and Alex had been discussing for the last month. But Alex was already halfway out of the door.

'Yes, okay. Maybe we can sit down together later today to go through some things?'

'That would be great.' He flashed her a sudden smile. 'You like your office?'

'It's better than I could have imagined. Thank you so much, Alex.'

'My pleasure.' He turned, closing the door behind him.

Marie leaned back in her chair, listening to the silence. There was a lot to do here. A whole community of health professionals to build. There were mountains to move, and the most stubborn of them had just walked downstairs. Alex had built his dream, and although he had a fierce determination to see it thrive, Marie sensed he couldn't love it.

That was going to have to change.

After Saturday's quiet solitude, most of which Alex had spent closeted in his office, the bustle of workmen and staff on Monday morning was a welcome relief. Marie spent two days with Sofia Costa, the practice manager, interviewing the shortlisted candidates for the medical support team, and on Wednesday morning picked up the flowering plant she'd brought from home and went down to Alex's office.

She'd wondered if his subdued manner was a reaction to their kiss, part of some kind of attempt to keep things professional, but he was like that with everyone. Thoughtful, smiling, but without the spark that made him Alex. In one way it was a relief to find that it wasn't just her, but it was clear that the change in Alex's life and the months spent developing this place had taken their toll on him. He normally thrived on hard work, but this was different. It seemed to be draining all the life out of him.

'The interviews went well?' He looked up from the pile of paperwork on his desk.

'Very well. It was difficult to decide, as they were all good candidates. But Sofia and I have chosen three who are excellent. I've emailed their CVs to you so you can take a look at them.'

She put the Busy Lizzie plant down on his desk and Alex picked it up, examining the bright red flowers. 'Is this a subtle hint that my office could do with brightening up?'

'No, I don't do subtle. It's more in the way of a brazen, in-your-face hint.'

Alex smiled, walking over to the windowsill and putting the pot at the centre. He moved it to one side and then the other, finding the place he wanted it.

'I don't suppose you have any more of these, do you?'

Marie hid her smile. The old Alex was still there—he just needed a bit of coaxing out. If he wanted more plants she'd fill his windowsill with colour.

'I've got loads at home. I took some cuttings from my mum's. I'll bring you more tomorrow.'

'Thanks.'

'I've got an idea.' She sat down in one of the chairs on the other side of his desk.

'Fire away.'

His lips curved a little. Alex clearly hadn't lost his penchant for ideas of all shapes and sizes.

'The light wells. They're pretty awful as they are, and I'd like to turn them into gardens. I spoke to Jim Armitage and he says that there are some brick pavers that were taken up from around the gym and he saved because they were still good. He reckons they should be fine on top of the concrete, but he needs to get out there to check everything. The key card lock disengages, but there's an original lock still on the door. Jim was going to climb out of the window, but I persuaded him not to.'

The foreman of works was a portly man approaching retirement, and Marie had feared he'd either get stuck while climbing out or not be able to get back in again. The same thing had obviously occurred to Alex, because one of those flashes of humour that reminded Marie so painfully of the man he'd once been lit his face.

'Good call. I might have the key somewhere...' He opened the bottom drawer of his desk, producing a large cardboard box full of keys of all shapes and sizes.

'So you'll come and have a look with me?'

If Alex was going to tell her that she was quite capable of doing this alone, then she was going to have to argue with him. She was capable, but that wasn't the point.

'I have a few things to do...'

'This is much more important, Alex. As your co-director, I'm telling you that you need to come.'

He grinned suddenly and stood up.

Step one accomplished. Step two might be a bit trickier...

Marie never had been much good at hiding the motives behind her actions. It was something Alex wished he hadn't had to learn how to do. She'd decided to get him out of his office and there was no point in arguing that he had work to do when Marie was determined. And when Alex thought about it, he didn't really want to argue.

He'd missed this. Marie had brought colour to a life that had become suffused by restful cream

walls and spaces that were fit for purpose. He
followed her along the corridor that ran parallel
to one of the light wells, holding the box of keys.

She took her key card from her pocket, swip-
ing it to disengage the main lock, and then started
to fish around in the box for keys that looked as
if they might fit the older one. It took a few tries
to find one that fitted, but finally Alex heard a
click as the key turned in the lock.

She rattled the handle of the door. 'It's still
stuck…'

Alex tried the door. 'Looks as if it's been
painted shut—no one ever goes out there. You
want me to open it?'

She gave him a beatific smile. 'Yes, please.'

He put his shoulder to the door, and there was
a cracking sound as it opened. Marie picked up a
plastic bag, which had been sitting on one of the
windowsills, and stepped out into the courtyard.

'Right. We need to check the height of the pavers…' She produced a brick from the bag, wedg-
ing it under the bottom of the doorframe. 'That
looks okay to me. And Jim says there's drainage,
so we'll be fine there…'

She pulled a folded A2 sheet from the bag,
spreading it out on the stained concrete. Marie
was nothing if not prepared, and Alex was getting the feeling that he'd been set up. But Marie
did it so delightfully.

'I reckon seats there…and planters in groups here and here… Perhaps a small water feature in the centre? What do you think?'

'I think that's great. Do we have the budget for it?'

'Yes, if we don't go overboard with things and we use the resources that we already have. Jim says that one of his guys will take me to the garden centre to get what we need.'

'Fine.' But something told Alex that his agreement to the plan wasn't enough. Marie wanted more.

She turned to him, her eyes dancing with violet shards in the sunlight. 'What do you say, Alex? Do you want to make a garden with me?'

Suddenly the one thing that Alex wanted was to make a garden, but there were more pressing things on his agenda.

'Do you think that's the best use of our time? We're opening in six days.'

'And the clinic's ready. You're not, though. You've been stuck in your office, working seven days a week, for months. You need a break before we open, and since I doubt you'll go home and take one this is a good second-best.'

This. This was why he'd wanted Marie to be his co-director. For moments like now, when she glared at him and told him exactly what he was doing wrong. He'd hoped she might come up with a plan, and that it might not just be for the clinic but for him as well.

'Well?' She put her hands on her hips.

She was unstoppable, and Alex did need a break. Something to refill the well that felt in imminent danger of running dry.

'Okay. I'm in your hands. What do you want me to do?'

'I'll go and get what we need for this court-yard, and we can store it all in the other one and start planting everything up. I'll ask Jim exactly when he can lay the paving; he said he'd prob-ably be able to fit it in this week.'

'Maybe I can help with that. I could do with the exercise.' The waistband of his trousers was slightly tighter than usual, and Alex reckoned that he really needed to get to the gym.

'I wasn't going to mention that.'

Her gaze fell to his stomach, and Alex instinc-tively sucked in a breath. He hadn't thought he was *that* out of shape.

'It's nothing a little sunshine and activity won't fix.'

'What? You're my personal trainer now?'

'Someone has to do it, Alex. What are friends for?

This was exactly what friends were for. Crash-ing into your day like a shaft of light, slicing through the cobwebs. Doing something unexpected that turned an average working week into an adventure.

Alex dismissed the thought that it was also what lovers were for. He'd never had a lover who meant as much to him as his friend Marie. He doubted he ever would. He'd seen the way his father had reduced his mother to a sad, silent ghost. Alex had decided a long time ago that he would concentrate on making the best of every other aspect of his life and pass on marriage and a family.

He caught her just as she was leaving the clinic with Eammon, one of Jim Armitage's builders. 'Don't worry about the budget on this. Get whatever you want. I'll cover it.'

Marie shook her head. 'We have the money to buy a few planters and grow things. It's better that way.'

He'd said the wrong thing again. It would mean nothing to him to buy up a whole garden centre. It occurred to Alex that he was becoming used to throwing money at any problem that presented itself, because that meant much less to him than his time. He hadn't realised he'd lost so much of himself.

'Okay, well...' He'd play it her way. 'Let me know when you get back and I'll help unload the van.'

'Great. Thanks.' She gifted him with an irrepressible smile and turned, hurrying across to the front gates, her red dress swirling around her legs.

As she climbed up into the front seat of the builder's van that was parked outside the gates, Alex couldn't help smiling. Marie always looked gorgeous, but somehow she seemed even more so now, rushing towards a future that held only excitement for her and looking oddly pristine in the dusty, battered vehicle.

She'd be a couple of hours at least. Alex turned back to his office, feeling suddenly that those two hours were going to drag a little, with only a desk full of paperwork to amuse him.

When Marie returned, Alex had already found the key to the other courtyard and opened it up, then changed into the jeans and work boots that he kept in the office for inspecting the works in progress with Jim.

The van pulled into the car park, and Marie climbed down from the front seat, cheeks flushed with excitement.

'You got everything?'

'Yes, we've got some small shrubs and loads of seeds, along with planters and growing compost. I came in two pounds under budget.'

'And you didn't buy yourself an ice cream?' Alex walked to the back of the van, waiting for Eammon to open the doors.

'*I* bought her an ice cream.'

Eammon grinned, and Alex wished suddenly that he'd volunteered to drive. He'd missed his chance to play the gentleman.

He started to haul one of the heavy bags of compost out of the back of the van, finding that it was more effort than he'd expected to throw it over his shoulder. He and Eammon stacked the bags in the courtyard while Marie unloaded the planters from the van.

'What do you think? I was hoping that less might be more.'

She'd arranged some of the planters in a group and was surveying them thoughtfully. There was a mix of colours and styles. Some large clay pots, a few blue-glazed ones, which were obviously the most expensive, and some recycled plant tubs, which were mostly grey but contained random swirls of colour. Each brought out the best in the others.

'They're going to look great.'

Alex picked up two of the heavier clay pots and Eammon took the pot that Marie had picked up, telling her to bring the lighter plastic tubs through.

Another opportunity for gallantry missed. Alex had carefully avoided any such gestures, reckoning that they might be construed as being the result of the kiss that they'd both decided to ignore, but he reckoned if they were okay for Eammon then they were probably permissible for him, too.

Alex was clearly struggling with his role at the clinic. If he'd worked for this then he would have seen it as the realisation of a lifetime's ambition, but it had all fallen so easily into his lap. The inheritance had left him without anything to strive for and it was destroying him.

Marie's ambitions had always been small: helping her mother cope with the pressures of four young children and a job, then making a life for herself and keeping an eye on her younger brothers. But at least they were simple and relatively easily fulfilled.

After they'd unloaded the van, carrying everything through to the courtyard and stacking it neatly, Alex seemed in no particular hurry to get back to his office. Marie asked him if he wanted to help and he nodded quietly.

She set out the seed trays, filling them with compost, and Alex sorted through the packets. Then they got to work, sitting on a pair of upturned crates that Alex had fetched.

'So…tell me again what country your great-grandfather was the king of?'

They'd worked in near silence for over an hour, and now that everyone had gone home for the evening they were alone. Marie had been regretting her reaction to Alex's disclosure about his family, and the subject had become a bit of a no-go area between them.

Alex looked up at her questioningly. 'It doesn't matter. It doesn't exist any more.'

'I'm just curious. And… I feel sorry about giving you a hard time when you told me about it.'

'It's nothing.' He puffed out breath and then relented. 'Belkraine. My great-grandfather was Rudolf the Most Excellent and Magnificent, King of Belkraine. Modesty doesn't run in the family.'

'I guess if you've got a few squillion in cash and a palace then you don't need to be modest…' She paused. 'Did he have a palace?'

'Why stop at one when you can have several? The old Summer Palace still exists; it's near the border between Austria and Italy.'

'Have you ever been there?'

His lip curled slightly. 'It was my father's idea of a summer holiday. We'd go there every year, for a tour of what was supposed to be our birthright. It was excruciating.'

Alex sounded bitter. He wasn't a man who held on to bad feelings, so this must be something that ran deep with him.

'I'd be interested to see where my ancestors lived. Although I can say pretty definitely that it wasn't in a palace.'

'I guess it's an interesting place. It's been restored now, and it's very much the way it was when my great-grandparents lived there. Unfortunately my father used to insist on pointing at everything and telling my mother and me in a very loud voice that all this was really ours and that we'd been exiled to a life of poverty.'

'Ouch.'

Marie pulled a face and his lips twitched into something that resembled a smile.

'Yes, ouch. Even though my great-grandfather brought a fair bit of the family's wealth with him—and we had more than enough—my father used to reckon that he was poor because he didn't have everything he thought he should. He had no idea what real poverty is. It was just... embarrassing.'

'Is that why you never said anything about it?' Marie was beginning to understand that this hadn't been a wish to deceive, but something that had hurt him very badly.

'That and a few hundred other things. Like having to wear a version of the Crown Prince's military uniform at the annual party he gave on the anniversary of our family ascending the throne in 1432. After a particularly bloody series of wars, I might add. My family took the kingdom from someone else, so I never could see how having it taken from us was any cause for complaint.'

He ripped open a seed packet as if he was trying to chop its head off. Seeds scattered all over the concrete and Alex shook his head in frustration, cursing under his breath.

Marie swallowed down the temptation to tell him that it was okay, that they could pick them up again. This wasn't about the seeds, and he'd obviously not had much chance to get it out of his system. The idea that it had been nagging at him for so many years, concealed beneath the carefree face he'd shown to the world, was unbearably sad.

She bent down, picking the seeds up one by one. 'Good thing these aren't begonias. We'd never be able to pick up those tiny seeds.'

He laughed, his resentment seeming to disappear suddenly. Marie would rather he held on to it. His feelings were shut away now, under lock and key, and when he'd tipped the last of the seeds back into the packet, he stood.

'I've a few things that I really need to do. Do you mind if we start again in the morning?'

'Of course not. Anything I can give you a hand with?'

'No, stay here. We really need a garden. It will give people hope.'

Would it give *him* hope? Or just other people?

Marie decided not to ask, because Alex was already opening the door that led back into the building, and she doubted whether he would have answered anyway.

CHAPTER FOUR

WAS THIS REALLY what Marie wanted to know about him? That he was the great-grandson of a tyrant king? Alex decided he was overreacting, and that it was just natural curiosity. *He'd* be curious about the mechanics of the thing if he'd suddenly found out that Marie was a fairy princess. But then that wouldn't come as much of a surprise—he'd always rather suspected that she was.

He waited until he heard the main doors close and then threw down his pen. The table of dependencies he'd been sketching out for Jim Armitage wasn't working anyway, and he should probably just tell him what needed to be finished before the clinic opened, and leave him to work it out. There was such a thing as being too hands-on. And he couldn't leave without taking a look...

Marie had moved some of the planters, obviously having changed her mind on how best to group them. The shrubs were arranged under a makeshift plastic canopy to protect them from the weather, along with the seed trays that they'd filled.

Alex sat down on the upturned crate he'd occupied earlier. It occurred to him that this was the first garden he'd ever really had a hand in. His parents' garden had been designed to be looked at, preferably from a distance, and hadn't really been the kind of place for a child who might disturb its well-ordered beauty. When he'd left home, the indoor plants he'd bought to brighten up his flat had generally died from neglect, and Alex had decided that his contribution to the environment was to leave them in the shop and let them go to someone who would remember to water them.

But this time the idea of creating something from scratch and tending it over time was something he very much wanted to be a part of. And so what if Marie had asked him about the one thing he always shrank from discussing? She wanted to know about the Kings of Belkraine because she wanted to know about him. If she had any questions tomorrow, he'd answer them.

When he arrived at the clinic the next morning, Marie was already sitting on her crate, wearing a T-shirt and jeans. His crate had been left in exactly the same place it had occupied last night, in mute invitation.

Alex opened the door of the courtyard and went to sit opposite her.

'Morning.'

She gave him a bright smile. Her cheeks were still a little red from where the sun had kissed them yesterday.

Alex nodded and sat down, reaching for an empty seed tray from the pile. He filled the tray with compost and opened one of the seed packets, letting the cool quiet of the hour before everyone else arrived for work seep into him for a while before he spoke.

'I argued with my father and he threw me out of the house when I was eighteen.'

She looked up at him, her lip quivering. 'That's a hard thing to have to bear, Alex.'

He shook his head. Marie knew far more about hardship than he did. 'Your father left when you were ten.'

'It's not a competition, Alex. You don't have to keep quiet about what happened to you because you think what happened to me might have been worse—it doesn't work that way. Anyway, my father left because of what happened between my mum and him. She told us that. It's different.'

Alex wondered how different it really was. Marie had worked so hard to help support her brothers, and he'd always had a sense that she felt somehow responsible for her father leaving.

But this wasn't about probing her; Marie had never made any secret of her childhood. He'd hidden his past out of a wish to leave it behind.

Now, for the sake of the friendship that was so precious to him, he had to put that right.

'What did you argue about?' Marie had clearly been waiting for him to go on, and finally she asked the question.

'My father was an embittered man. He had everything money could buy, but he considered that our family had been deprived of its birthright. He insisted that we live as if we *were* royal, but I wanted more from life than that. I wanted to make my own choices. I wanted to be a doctor. He told me that if I went to medical school he'd disinherit me, and I told him to go ahead and do it.'

A faint smile hovered at Marie's lips. 'I wouldn't have expected you to do anything else. Didn't he ever see what you'd achieved and come around?'

'No, he never accepted what I wanted to do. The money that took me through medical school was from a trust that my grandfather had set up for me. He knew what my father was like, and he locked the trust in an ironclad agreement so my father couldn't get his hands on it.'

'Would he have tried? It sounds as if he had enough already.' Marie's eyebrows shot up.

'My father didn't care about the money; he thought it a paltry amount. He wanted control over me. I got to do what I wanted when I was eighteen because of that trust.'

'So being disinherited...that was a good thing in a way. Your father couldn't force you into his mould.'

'I felt as if I was free.'

She chuckled, picking up another seed tray. 'Free was how you seemed then. I used to envy you for it, but I didn't know what you'd had to go through to get your freedom. Did you never reconcile with your father?'

'I didn't want to. He was never a good husband; he hurt my mother very badly. I couldn't forgive him for that.'

There was nothing like telling a story to find out which parts of it really hurt. Alex could feel his chest tightening from the pain.

'Alex...?'

Marie was leaning forward now, concern registering on her face. Maybe she knew that this was what he really needed to say.

'He had mistresses. Lots of them. He used to spend a couple of nights a week in London, and my mother always seemed so sad. When I was little I thought she must miss him, but by the time I was fifteen I knew what was going on. He didn't go to much trouble to hide it.'

Marie's hand flew to her mouth. 'Your poor mother...'

'She just accepted it. That was the thing that hurt the most. She grew thinner and sadder every year, until finally she just seemed to fade away. She died five years ago.'

'And you never got to see her?'

'I used to visit her all the time. I'd call her, and she'd tell me when my father would be out of the house and I could come. It was the only thing she ever defied him over and she used to love hearing about what I was doing as a doctor. She knew that she always had a home with me, but she'd never leave him.'

'People…they make their own decisions. Parents included.' Marie shot him a wry smile.

'Yeah.'

Alex had made his decision too. However much the idea of a wife and a family might appeal to him in theory, his parents' unhappy marriage had always made him balk at the prospect of commitment. His father's money and title were new reasons to make him wary. Alex didn't know how he was going to cope with that yet, and the last thing he wanted to do was inflict his own struggle on anyone else.

'I did try to speak to my father once—at my mother's funeral. It was a very lavish affair, and after the way he'd treated her it made me feel sick. But I decided that it was what she would have wanted, and so I went up to him to shake his hand. He turned his back on me. I'll never know why he changed his mind about leaving me his money and I wish he hadn't.'

Marie frowned at him suddenly. 'It sounds as if he did the right thing, for once.'

'What? You think I'm *better* as a billionaire king in exile?'

'No, I think you're pretty rubbish at it, actually.'

The tension in his shoulders began to dissolve and Alex grinned at her. 'That's one of the things I like about you. That you don't think it's a good thing.'

'I didn't say it wasn't a good thing. I said you were rubbish at it. Look around you and tell me it's not a good thing.'

'Point taken. So the clinic's a good thing and I'm a rubbish king. Is that right?'

She nodded. 'You can write your own script, Alex. If you let the money and the title define you then maybe that's what your father wanted. But if you define it, then you can do anything. Things ordinary people only dream of.'

As usual, Marie was right. He'd been letting the money and the title define him a little too much recently, and the idea that he could become anything he wanted lifted a weight from his shoulders. And right now he wanted to be a gardener.

Marie had finished planting three seed trays and they were lined up on one side of her. He hadn't completed any yet. Alex picked up his tray.

'I was wondering if you'd cover for me in the office. Today and tomorrow.' He finished planting the tray and laid it down next to hers.

'Yes, of course. You're going out?'

'No, I spoke with Jim Armitage and he's given me the go-ahead to lay the pavers. I've never done anything like that before, but...' He shrugged.

'You can learn. I don't think it's that difficult.' Marie's sudden smile told him what she thought of the idea.

'You don't mind, then?'

It had been Marie's idea for him to get involved with the garden, and now he was going one better.

'Mind?' Marie laughed, a clear happy sound that echoed slightly against the walls that surrounded them. 'Do I mind you getting covered in brick dust and sand while I sit in a nice comfortable office? Nah, I don't mind that at all.'

Marie had spent most of the morning in her office, trying to find things to do. When three-thirty came around and the stream of mothers walking past the clinic from the school began to start she fetched the printed leaflets which detailed the services the clinic had to offer from the stockroom, along with one of the chairs from the café, and went to sit out in the sun by the main gates.

It would be one thing if Alex had changed over a few years—everyone changed. But he'd always carried this burden. The pressure of inheriting the money after his father's death had just made him less adept at hiding it.

And she'd never noticed. Caught up in her own work and looking after her family, she'd seen Alex as someone she wished she could be. A golden dream that she'd held on to, wanting to believe that work and responsibility weren't the only things in life. But now she'd seen a new Alex, challenging and complicated, and she couldn't help loving him better for it.

The stream of parents and kids had lessened now, and she'd given away almost all her leaflets. She'd catch the two young mums who were dawdling down the road towards her, plastic bags hanging from the arms of their pushchairs, and then she'd call it a day.

'Hi. May I give you a leaflet, please? About what we're doing here...'

One of them nodded, taking the leaflet and stuffing it into one of her shopping bags. The other took hers, and started to read it.

'I was wondering what was happening with this place. I used to go to school here…'

'Me too.' Marie grinned. 'Looks a lot better now.'

'Tell me about it. It was a real dump when I came here. We transferred over to the new school after a year.'

'We're opening next week. You're welcome to come and have a look around, see how it's changed.'

'I don't know…' The woman shook her head.

'You don't have to sign up for anything. Just look. There's a café.' Marie fished in her pocket for one of the printed vouchers. 'And this is for a free coffee.'

The woman took the voucher, stowing it away in her purse. 'Okay, thanks. What do you think, Nisha?'

Marie offered a second voucher and Nisha took it. Now that she had a conversation going, Marie decided that she should capitalise on it.

'I don't suppose you'd like a few extra leaflets, would you? To give to your friends? We have a range of services.' Marie pointed to the list on the leaflet. 'There's going to be a gym and a swimming pool, and they'll be open seven days a week. There's a nominal charge for those, but we've tried to keep it affordable.'

'I used to like swimming. The pool over on Stratton Road closed down, you know.'

Two pairs of eyes suddenly focussed away from her and over her left shoulder. Marie turned and saw Alex, wheeling a barrow full of bricks around the side of the building.

'That's the director of the clinic.'

Nisha's eyebrows shot up and the other woman choked with laughter. 'Really? Doesn't mind getting his hands dirty, then?'

'When he's not laying bricks he's a doctor. But we don't just tackle specific medical problems— it's all about living well.'

'And what do you do here?'

'I'm a doctor too.'

'Neesh…?'

The other woman nudged her companion, but Nisha shook her head. A sixth sense pricked at the back of Marie's neck. This was just the kind of thing the clinic was here for—the problems that people didn't want to talk about.

'Take my card.' Marie offered one of the cards that had been printed with her name. 'If there's ever anything I can help with, just ask for me.'

Nisha nodded, taking the card. She looked at it, glanced at Marie, and then unzipped her handbag, putting the card inside. Maybe she'd take the offer up, but Marie knew from experience that she needed to let her think about it. Pushing now would only elicit a *no*.

'My name's Marie.' She turned to the other woman.

'Carol. Do you do mother-and-toddler swimming classes?'

'Yes—you can sign up for them next week, when the clinic opens.'

'I'll definitely do that. We come past here every day. We might get another eyeful of that director of yours…' Carol laughed as Nisha raised her eyebrows. 'Only joking, Neesh.'

The toddler in Carol's pushchair started to fret. 'Yeah, all right, Georgie. We'll be home soon, and then we're going to the park. It was nice to meet you, Marie.'

'You too. Hope I'll see you again soon.'

The two women started to walk again, chatting companionably. Marie heard footsteps behind her and turned to see Alex, holding two glasses of lemonade. He handed her one.

'Thanks, I could do with that. I've talked my head off, given out a whole handful of leaflets and also some free coffee vouchers. How are you doing?'

Alex grinned, leaning towards her as if he was about to impart something highly confidential. 'Rather well, I think.'

'Can I see it?'

'No. The courtyards are my territory for the next couple of days. You can have the offices and the front gates. I'll water the seeds for you.'

'You won't forget? You know how bad you are at watering plants.' Marie shot him an imploring look.

'That's reassuring. I'm expecting people to put their lives in my hands, and you can't trust me with a few seed trays.'

It was nice to see Alex teasing again. Marie had missed that, and it seemed that a little practical work had lifted some of the weight from his shoulders. He was looking a lot more like the relaxed and cheerful Alex that she'd known before all this had happened.

Alex nodded at the pavement behind her and Marie saw Carol hurrying towards them. It looked as if she had something on her mind.

'Hey, Carol. This is Alex, our director.'

'Pleased to meet you.'

Alex wiped his hand on his jeans and held it out. Carol shook it, nodding at him quickly, and then turned to Marie.

'Did you mean what you said? To Nisha?'

'About coming to see me? Of course. Is there something wrong?'

Carol nodded, tight-lipped.

'Do you want to come inside and talk?'

Perhaps it was something Carol didn't want to say in front of Alex.

'No. No, that's all right. I've got to get home—this one's going to start playing up in a minute.' She gestured down at Georgie, who was wriggling in the pushchair, clearly cross that the park was on hold for the moment.

Alex squatted down on his heels and poked his tongue out at the toddler. Their game of pulling faces seemed to be keeping them both occupied for a moment, which left Carol free to talk with Marie.

'Is there something Nisha needs? Something we can help with?'

'Yeah. Look, I can't really talk about it...'

Carol was almost whispering now, and Marie lowered her voice too.

'That's okay. Has she been to see her GP?'

'No, she won't. This place looks...' Carol shrugged. 'She might come here. I could get her to come. But you will see her, won't you? I don't know that it's a strictly medical thing.'

'If it's not a medical problem I'll refer her to someone who can help her. The whole point of this place is to find whatever answer is appropriate.'

'Right. Thanks. When are you opening? For... um...whatever... Appointments?'

'Next week. But Nisha doesn't need an appointment—she can come at any time. All you need to do is get her here and I'll make time to see her.'

'Great. Thanks.' Carol looked down at Georgie, who was laughing and trying to reproduce the faces Alex was making. 'I'd better get back. I told Nisha I was just popping back for something at the shops and I'd meet her in the park.'

'All right. But, Carol…' Marie caught Carol's arm before she could leave. 'This is important. If you think Nisha's in danger in any way you must get her to call someone. Or bring her here.'

'No, it's nothing like that. Her husband's a good man. It's just…embarrassing. You know?'

'Okay. I can do embarrassing. Get her to come and see me—you can come with her if that helps.' She glanced down at Alex, raising her voice to catch his attention. 'I don't think Alex's quite used up his stock of funny faces.'

Alex grinned up at Carol, getting to his feet. 'He's a great little chap.'

'Thanks. He can be a bit of a handful.' Carol was smiling now. 'I'll see you, then…?'

'I hope so.' Alex gave her a smile and Carol turned and hurried away.

'What was all that about?'

Marie shrugged. 'I don't know. Something about the friend she was with a moment ago. She wouldn't say.'

'You think she's in any danger?' Alex's first question was the same as Marie's had been. It was always their first question.

'No, Carol says it's embarrassing.'

He nodded, tipping his glass towards hers. 'Here's to your first patient, then. Congratulations, you've pipped me to the post. I haven't got any yet.'

'Thank you. I dare say that'll change, but I'm quietly triumphant over having beaten my excellent and glorious co-director.'

Marie took a sip of her lemonade and saw the corners of Alex's mouth quirk downwards. Maybe the joke was a little too close to the mark for him.

'All right. Never say that again.' His face was serious for a moment, and then he smiled, knowing he'd fooled her. 'I might consign you to the dungeons.'

'How about Your Majesty? I suppose that's out as well?'

He chuckled. 'Definitely. That's a throwing-from-the-battlements thing...'

'Get back to work, Alex.' Marie drained her glass, handing it back to him.

CHAPTER FIVE

MARIE HAD MADE no secret of the fact that staying away from the courtyards was driving her insane with curiosity. Alex had escorted her off the premises at five o'clock and gone back to work, sorting out the best of the bricks and discarding those that were damaged.

The second day of Alex's practical introduction to laying pavers had involved an early start and a concentrated burst of work, but by the afternoon he was surveying the newly swept paving with Charlie, the lad Jim Armitage had sent to help him. Alex suspected Charlie had also been instructed to report back to Jim if it looked as if he was about to make a complete mess of things, and it was a matter of some pride to him that Charlie hadn't gone to seek out his boss at any point.

'What do you think, Charlie?'

Charlie nodded sagely. 'Nice job. Are we going to lay out the planters now?'

'Yes, I think so. Then we can show it to Marie.'

'She can put her flowers in. She'll like that.'

Charlie spoke with the certainty of all his nineteen years, and Alex smiled. The warm colours of the brick had made all the difference to the space.

'Yes, I think she will. Thanks for all your hard work.'

Charlie nodded, obviously pleased.

They set out the planters from the chart Marie had given them, and Alex left Charlie to bring some of the shrubs through from the other court-yard while he went to find Marie.

She was sitting in the reception area, where she could keep an eye out for anyone whose cu-riosity had brought them to the door, staring at the screen of her laptop.

As soon as she saw him she jumped to her feet. 'Is it finished?'

'Yes. You want to come and see it?'

'There are a few things I have to do, but I'll have a look later on...' Alex's face must have shown his dismay and she laughed. 'Of *course* I want to come and see it!'

'Okay.' From his pocket he produced the extra-large handkerchief he'd brought from home that morning, brushing a speck of brick dust from it. 'Stand still for a moment.'

'You're going to blindfold me? Seriously?'

'Charlie's worked hard on this. I think it de-serves a little bit of a ceremony, don't you?'

The blindfold was nothing to do with Charlie.

Alex just wanted to see the look on Marie's face when she saw the paved courtyard.

'Yes, okay, then. Hurry up!'

He tied the blindfold carefully over her eyes, trying not to breathe in the scent of her hair. Then, just for good measure, he turned her around a couple of times. Marie flung out her hand, her fingers brushing his chest, before they found a secure hold on the sleeve of his T-shirt. Alex shivered as tingles pulsed down his spine. They were almost in an embrace.

'Enough, Alex! Take me there or else!'

'Okay. Hold my arm.'

She clung on to him as he walked her slowly along the corridor. When the idea of blindfolding her had occurred to him this morning Alex hadn't taken into consideration how good it would feel to have her walking so close, hanging on to him. He was glad he hadn't foreseen it, because if he had he might have thought better of the idea. And it would have been a shame to miss this moment.

Charlie opened the door for them, standing back with a huge grin on his face.

'The step's right in front of you...' Alex held her arm firmly so she couldn't fall, and Marie extended her foot. 'That's it. A little further.'

When her foot hit the surface of the bricks she gave a shiver of anticipation, her fingers tightening around his arm. Alex's knees almost gave way, and then suddenly his body was taut and strong again, ready to catch her if she fell.

Marie stepped out into the courtyard carefully, letting him lead her into its centre.

'You can take the blindfold off now.' He heard his voice catch on the lump in his throat and knew he dared not do it for her. If he touched her hair again he might forget himself.

Marie reached up, fumbling a little with the knot. She was silent for a moment, her hand to her mouth as she looked around.

'Herringbone! I didn't expect that!'

Alex and Charlie exchanged smug looks. The herringbone pattern meant that there had been extra work in cutting the bricks at the edges, but they'd both agreed it would be worth it. Now, it was definitely worth it.

'This is *beautiful*. It's perfect. Charlie, you must have worked so hard…'

It was just like Marie to praise the younger member of the team first. Charlie had worked hard, he'd made sure everything was exactly right, and he deserved it. Alex smiled as Charlie's cheeks began to redden.

'And you've set out all my planters as well. Thank you so much.'

Charlie nodded. 'Would you like to see the drainage gulley?'

'Yes, please.'

Alex watched as Charlie led her to one corner of the courtyard, showing her where excess rainfall would drain away from the surface and into a waste pipe.

'You've made such a good job of it. When we put some flowers and seating out here it's going to be a lovely place for people to sit.'

Charlie was grinning from ear to ear, and had obviously taken about as much praise as one young man could stand from a beautiful woman. He muttered something about having to report back to Jim, and made his escape. Then Marie turned her gaze onto Alex.

No words. Just a smile. But Alex felt just as pleased with her reaction as Charlie had obviously been.

'You like it?'

'You really need to ask, Alex? I love it.'

Alex nodded. This was everything he needed. It was well worth the hard manual labour, the aching muscles and the scraped fingers.

'Our garden…' Marie turned around as if she could see it right now. Flowers and seating— everything as it would be when it was finished.

'Yes. I like the sound of that.'

'Me too. I could really, really hug you. If you weren't so dirty.'

He could really, really hug her too, and love every second of it. It was just as well that he was covered in grime, with streaks of adhesive all over his jeans.

'I think I'll go and give the showers in the gym changing rooms a trial run. Then I'll go to my office.'

'This has been keeping you from your other work…' Marie shot him a guilty look.

'There's nothing so urgent that it won't wait until tomorrow. I just really need to sit down.'

'Then come out here. I'll fetch you a chair and a cold drink, and you can sit and watch me work.'

The idea was much more enchanting than it should be. He could survey his handiwork with a sense of pride at something started and finished amongst a list of tasks that never seemed to end. Better still, he could watch Marie. Her dress brought a splash of colour to the monotonous pale walls of the clinic, and the way she moved injected life and fluidity. He loved the way the light glinted in her hair and—

Enough. He should confine himself to appreciating the colours of the brick. He might even allow himself a moment of self-congratulation that all that tapping with a mallet had borne fruit and they were perfectly level.

'I'll be back in ten minutes.'

He grinned at her, leaving her standing in the middle of the courtyard, still looking around, while he headed for the shower.

* * *

Marie couldn't wait to get started. By the time Alex had returned she'd brought the rest of the pots and seed trays through from the other courtyard and was shifting the planters around into different configurations.

'Stop!' Alex was leaning back in his seat, drinking lemonade. 'That's the one I like.'

Marie stood back. 'Yes, me too. Then there's space for some seating.'

Alex nodded. 'Where are you thinking of getting that from?'

Now or never... The idea had occurred to her yesterday, and since then Marie hadn't been able to stop thinking about it. 'I had my eye on some old garden benches I saw in a junk shop. They'd scrub up nicely. But...'

Suddenly she felt as if it was too much to ask. As if this little garden with its recycled pots and bedding plants grown from seed wasn't really good enough.

'But what?'

Marie must have shown her embarrassment, because Alex was suddenly still, looking at her thoughtfully. There was no way out now...

'I thought... Did your mother like flowers?'

He raised his eyebrows in surprise. The question had come so much out of the blue.

'She loved her garden. She was always out

there, planting things and helping the gardener. Whenever my father wasn't around, that is. He reckoned she shouldn't get involved with any actual work.'

'I thought… Well, I know this garden's never going to make the Chelsea Flower Show, but you made it… And you know how they have seats in the park with people's names on them…?'

She couldn't quite say it, but Alex had caught her meaning and was nodding slowly. Marie held her breath, hoping Alex wouldn't take offence at the suggestion.

'My mother would have loved this garden. And I'd like to buy something for it in memory of her.'

Marie let out a sigh of relief. 'You're sure, Alex? I know it can't do your feelings for her justice.'

He shook his head. 'My father thought cut flowers and ostentatious wreaths did her justice. I hated her funeral and I wanted to go away and do something simple for her on my own, but I never could find the right thing. *This* is the right thing. You said you wanted a water feature?'

'Yes? Do you think that would be better than seating?'

'Much better. She liked the sound of water; she used to say it was soothing.' Alex thought for a moment. 'No brass plates with her name, though. I don't want that.'

His obvious approval for the idea gave Marie the courage to suggest another. 'What was her name?'

Hopefully it wasn't something too long...

'Elise.'

Perfect. 'If you wanted we might spell her name out? With the plants we choose to put around the water feature?'

He smiled suddenly. 'I'd love that. Thank you for thinking of her, Marie. She'd be so pleased to be part of this garden.'

'Good.' Marie's heart was beginning to return to something that resembled a normal pace. She felt almost light-headed.

'As this is Friday, and we'll be opening on Monday, I'll have to go to the garden centre this weekend. I don't suppose you could spare a couple of hours to help me choose?'

Marie rolled her eyes. 'Where else did you think I was going to be this weekend? Yes, of course I'll help you.'

They'd worked hard at the weekend. Alex had chosen an old millstone, with water bubbling from the centre of it, which was a great deal heavier and more expensive than Marie had envisaged. Jim was going to have to construct a base for it, and install the motor and drainage tank, but Alex and Marie had heaved the millstone into the place reserved for it in the court-yard, and it already looked stunning.

She hadn't stopped Alex from buying plants, some more planters for them, and four wooden benches. This was a labour of love, and the look in his eyes when they'd hauled the first of the planters through into the garden, filled it with compost and arranged echinacea and lavender in it had told her that it meant a great deal more to him than anything money could buy.

On Monday morning everything was ready. Tina, the receptionist, was at her post, and Alex and Marie were sitting in the chairs at the far end of the reception area, along with one of the counsellors, a physiotherapist, and therapists from the pool and the gym. Tina would welcome visitors and summon the relevant person to talk to them.

'You're sure we shouldn't be next to Tina? She looks a bit on her own.' Alex waved across to Tina, who waved cheerily back.

'No. We don't want to frighten anyone away with a horde of therapists waiting to pounce.'

'But I *want* to pounce. Actually, I want to go out onto the street and kidnap anyone who walks by.' Alex was looking a little like a caged lion at the moment.

'Well you can't. We're supposed to be friendly

and non-intimidating. We wait, Alex. We've got some groups coming soon. Before you know it you'll have more people than you can cope with.'

'I hope so...' He caught his breath, stiffening suddenly as a shadow fell across the entrance. 'Aren't they the women you were talking to the other day?'

Carol and Nisha had manoeuvred their push-chairs into the lobby and were standing by the door, looking around. They moved forward to let a group of young mums past, who had obviously just dropped their children off at school.

'Yes.' Marie smirked at him. 'They're mine, Alex. You can wait here until Tina calls you...'

He grinned at her, obviously relieved that the reception area was beginning to fill up. 'No one likes an overachiever, Marie.'

'Too bad. I'm still first.'

She stood up, walking across to where Carol and Nisha were standing.

'Hi, Marie.' Carol saw her first, and gave her a wave. 'We've come to check out the mum-and-baby swimming classes.'

'That's great. I'll get you signed up... Would you like to come and see the pool first? It's in the old gym.'

'The gym?' Carol rolled her eyes. 'That I'd love to see.'

Marie led the way. Both women had been to

school here, and by the time they got to the swimming pool the three of them were swapping memories of their years spent here.

'You've worked wonders with it all, that's for sure.' Carol nodded her head in approval of the changing rooms and showers, and then stopped short when Marie opened the door that led through to the pool area. 'Wow! This is a bit different!'

The aqua blues and greens of the tiles and the light playing across the water made this one of Marie's favourite parts of the clinic. 'This is the main exercise pool. The hydrotherapy pool is where we're holding the mum-and-baby classes.'

'Does it matter if I can't swim?' Nisha was looking uncertainly at the pool.

'No, the hydrotherapy pool is much shallower than this one. You'll be able to stand up in it. It's kept at a warmer temperature, which makes it more suitable for babies and children.'

Marie led the way through to the smaller pool, where the same blue-and-green tones lent a more restful, intimate atmosphere. Georgie whooped with joy and started to wriggle in his pushchair, obviously keen to try it out straight away.

'I think that's one taker!' Carol grinned, taking him out of the pushchair and keeping a tight hold on him in case he decided to try and jump in. 'What do you think, Nisha?'

'Yes, definitely.'

The matter was settled. Marie had filled two places on the mother-and-baby swimming course, and maybe she'd get a chance to talk a bit more to Nisha.

'Would you like to come to the cafeteria for some coffee?'

'That would be nice. There was something I wanted to ask…' Nisha smiled hesitantly.

'Oh. Yes—good idea. I'll leave you to it, then. See you tomorrow, Nisha. Thanks for the tour, Marie.'

Georgie's protests went unheard as Carol put him back into the pushchair and hurried away, giving them both a wave.

Marie turned to Nisha, who was grinning broadly at her friend's receding figure. 'If there's something you want to talk about we could have coffee in my office.'

'It might not be anything at all. I'm probably just being silly…' Nisha twisted her mouth into a grimace.

'If it matters to you then it's something. The one thing I'm *not* going to do is tell you that you're being silly. You're the one who tells me what's important.'

Nisha nodded. 'It *is* important to me. I wish you could help me…'

* * *

Half an hour later Marie walked Nisha through to the reception area, which was now buzzing with activity. Nisha was grinning, clutching the information pack and the appointment card Marie had given her. Alex was nowhere to be seen, and it was another half hour before he appeared again.

'Everything okay with Nisha and Carol?'

'Yes, it's all good.'

She nodded towards his office, and by silent agreement they walked away from the bustle of people. Alex closed the door.

'I had a talk with Nisha; she says she hasn't felt right about sex since having her baby. She's worried about her relationship with her husband.'

He nodded. 'So what did you both decide?'

'Nisha's coming back to see me tomorrow. I'll examine her, and she's given me permission to write to her doctor so he can send her for some tests. Once we've ruled anything physical out we can discuss relationship therapy here.'

'She looked as if she was happy about that?'

'Yes—she said she'd get her husband to come with her tomorrow. He's tried to talk to her about it, but she says she panics and shuts him down.'

'Just talking about it helps.' He threw himself into his chair, staring at the ceiling. 'Of course, I'm a proven expert on talking about things.'

The heavy irony in his tone set off an alarm

bell. Something was up with Alex. His hand was shaking, and it didn't seem that hopeful nerves about their opening day was the cause.

'What's up?' She sat down.

'It's...' He waved his hand dismissively. 'Telling you it's nothing and that we should be getting back isn't going to wash, is it?'

'No. There are plenty of people out there to greet visitors, and we're confident the staff here can manage without us for ten minutes. Aren't we, Alex?'

'Yes. Absolutely.' He puffed out a breath. 'In that case... I had a boy who came in to ask about bodybuilding classes. He's only ten. I talked to him a bit, and told him that he'd have to bring one of his parents with him before he could sign up for any kind of exercise class with us.'

'Why did he want to do bodybuilding?' she asked, knowing Alex must have had the same instinct she did.

'It turned out that he'd skipped off school, so I got Tina to phone the school and they sent a teacher down to fetch him. He's being bullied.'

'Poor kid. And he wants to be able to fight back?'

'Yes. His teacher's going to talk to the parents, and I told her we would enrol him in our anti-bullying programme. He's a little overweight, so if he wants to do exercises then I'll get Mike to devise an exercise programme that suits his age and build.'

'That makes sense.'

'Yeah… But when he realised I wasn't just going to sign him up for bodybuilding he threw a tantrum and then…started to cry—' Alex's voice broke, suddenly.

'That's good, Alex. You got through to him. He must have a lot of negative emotion bottled up.'

Alex was committed to setting up a programme for both kids and adults who were being bullied. He'd applied his customary insight and thoroughness and then left it to a specialist.

Marie had supposed that someone with Alex's charm and natural leadership ability couldn't possibly have first-hand knowledge of being bullied, so he'd left the finer points to the experts he'd recruited. But she'd based her supposition on what she'd thought she knew about Alex. The happy childhood she'd imagined for him.

'You know, I always wanted you to have been happy as a child.'

He looked up at her. 'Yeah? That's nice.'

'Not really. I just wanted to know someone who'd grown up normally. It made me feel better—as if that was something I could shoot for.'

'Ah. Sorry to disappoint you, then.' He turned the corners of his mouth down.

'But, thinking about it, I guess it might have

been a bit difficult to make friends when you were little.'

He was gazing at his desk, as if something there might provide an answer. 'My father didn't think I should play with any of the kids who lived nearby because I was a prince. I was taught at home until it came time for me to be packed off to an exclusive boarding school. I was a shy kid, with a name that invited a thousand jokes. Of course I got bullied.'

And so he'd become the student who everyone liked. He'd listened to what people said and charmed them all. Marie had never looked past that.

'I wasn't much of a friend, was I?'

His eyebrows shot up. 'What? You were kind and honest. You brought me colour, and you showed me that however hard things are there's always time to celebrate the good things. I wanted...'

He fell silent suddenly, and in the warmth of his gaze Marie knew what he'd wanted. He'd wanted *her*. She'd wanted him too. Honesty was good—but this was one place they couldn't go.

'I wanted to be like you.'

His smooth refusal to face that particular fact was a relief, because Marie couldn't face it either. She'd never really moved on from wanting Alex.

'Will you do me a favour?' she asked.

'Anything.'

The look in his eyes told her he meant it.

'You've got a lot you can give to the anti-bully-ing programme. All those feelings and the things no one ever said. I want you to get more involved with it.'

He laughed suddenly. 'Don't underestimate me by giving me the easy option, will you.'

'You *want* me to underestimate you?'

'No, not really. Keeping me honest is what you do best.' He held his hands up in a gesture of smiling surrender. 'Yes, I'll do it. And now we really should be getting back to our visitors.'

CHAPTER SIX

YESTERDAY HAD BEEN a success. The flood of people who'd wanted to be first to explore the new clinic had subsided into a steady but satisfying trickle. Alex had received a couple of calls from local doctors, enquiring about referring patients to the clinic, and he'd shown a consultant from the nearby hospital around. She had a young patient whose family were currently travelling an hour each way to get to a hydrotherapy pool, and was pleased to find a closer facility that would meet the girl's needs.

Today there was a new challenge.

Alex assumed his best trust-me-I'm-a-doctor smile, and when he looked down at Marie he saw a similar one plastered uneasily across her face.

'Oh, really, Alex.' Sonya Graham-Hall flapped her hand at the photographer from the local paper, indicating that he was to stand down while she gave her clients a good talking-to. 'Can you try not to look as if you've eaten something that doesn't agree with you? You're supposed to be welcoming. And stand a little closer to Marie. You're a team...'

Marie was looking a little overawed by Sonya. Alex took a step towards her, feeling the inevitable thrill as her shoulder touched his arm. He bent towards her, whispering an old joke from medical school, and she suppressed a laugh. He couldn't help smiling, and heard the camera click rapidly.

'Wonderful!'

Sonya beamed at everyone, and Alex stepped forward to shake the photographer's hand and thank him. Then Sonya marched across the reception area to where the local reporter was standing, leading him towards the front doors.

'What's she doing?' Marie looked up at him. 'Can't he find his own way?'

'It's Sonya's modus operandi. She's making sure he knows what he's meant to write. Although he probably won't realise that's what she's done until after he's filed his story.'

Alex knew Sonya's husband from school, and knew she was the best PR representative in London. She was so much in demand that it was usual for her to interview clients, rather than the other way round. Alex had been lucky, though, and a phone call had not only managed to secure Sonya's services, but they were on a pro bono basis, because she loved the idea of the clinic. There was something to be said for the public school network.

'She's formidable, isn't she?' Marie's smile indicated that she thought formidable was a really good thing. 'I'm a little scared of her.'

Alex couldn't fathom what Marie would have to be scared about. If he'd been asked to define 'formidable', the first person who would have come to mind was Marie. But not quite in the same way as Sonya, who relied on killer heels, designer jackets and an upper-class accent that would have sliced through concrete.

'She knows so many important people...'

'It's her job to know people. Anyway, don't we prefer to think of *everyone* as important?'

Marie frowned, nudging him with her elbow. 'Of course we do. You know what I mean.'

Alex knew. Marie had already told him that she felt like a fish out of water with the great and the good, but they were exactly the kind of people who had the money and influence to help them make this project grow into a whole chain of clinics in different parts of the country. He wished Marie would stop thinking of them as somehow out of her league, because she was just as good as any of them.

'Right, then.' Sonya returned, beaming. 'I think he's on track. While I'm here, perhaps we can review where we are with everything else.'

'Thanks, Sonya. My office?'

Alex led the way, hearing Sonya chatting

brightly to Marie, and Marie's awkward, awe-struck replies.

Sonya plumped herself into one of the easy chairs, drawing a slim tablet out of her hand-bag. In Sonya's eyes, paper was messy, and she didn't do mess.

'Ooh, look. I love these. Such lovely colours. Can I have one?'

She leaned forward towards the coffee table, catching up the sheet of brightly coloured stickers that Marie had presented him with this morning. They had the name of the clinic on them, along with the main telephone number and website ad-dress, but Alex suspected that their real intent was to bring yet another much-needed shot of colour into his office.

'Help yourself. Marie has had a few printed. Shall we get some more?' Marie was already squirming in her seat, and Alex decided to em-barrass her a little more.

'Definitely. This is just the kind of fun thing we want. Something to get away from the bor-ing medical image.'

Alex felt his eyebrows shoot up.

'You know what I mean, Alex. Of course the medical part is the most important, but we want people to feel that you're approachable and not a stuffy old doctor.'

'Yes, we do.' Marie spoke up, reddening slightly at her audacity, and Sonya nodded.

'Now. I have the local radio interview set up— you're on your own with that one, Alex.'

'I can handle it.' Alex reckoned he could talk for ten minutes about the clinic easily enough.

'I'm sure you can. But I'm sending you a list of keywords and I want you to memorise them.'

Sonya swiped her finger across her tablet, and Alex heard a ding from the other side of the room as his desktop computer signalled that he had mail.

'Really? Keywords?'

'Yes, of course, darling. Think of it as like…' Sonya waved her hand in the air, groping for the right words.

'Like talking to a patient? Sometimes you have to emphasise what's important without confusing them with a load of irrelevant detail,' Marie ventured.

'Yes, exactly.'

Sonya gave Marie a conspiratorial smile, indicating she was pleased to see that at least one of them was on track, and Marie reddened again.

'I'm still working on the TV appearance, and there are a couple of functions that I'd like you to go to if I can get you an invitation.' Sonya leaned forward in her seat. 'You still have reservations about promoting the royal aspect in the media?'

Alex felt the side of his jaw twitch. 'If by *reservations* you mean that I'm absolutely sure that I don't want any of that in the media, then, yes, I'm still absolutely sure.'

'But it's such a good story, Alex. It would catch people's imaginations. It doesn't get much hotter than this—you're a doctor, very rich, royal, and to top it off a handsome bachelor.'

Alex shook his head, and then Marie spoke. Like an angel coming to rescue him.

'We've agreed a policy about this.'

'Ah… Yes?'

Sonya turned to Marie, clearly wanting her to elaborate. And Alex wanted to know what policy he'd agreed, as well.

'The compelling nature of Alex's story is the problem—it could quite easily prompt a media circus. Our values are that the clinic is the one and only important thing. Once it's a bit more established we could look at it again, but now's not the right time.'

Nicely said. Alex shot Marie a thankful look and she received it with the quiet graciousness of a queen.

Sonya nodded. 'Yes, that makes sense. Why didn't you say that before, Alex?'

'Marie sums it up a great deal better than I can.'

Sonya flashed him a look that told him she

agreed entirely with the sentiment, and then moved on. 'Now, I'm rather hoping you have something presentable to wear, Alex.'

'I have a suit…' Just the one. It was the suit he wore for job interviews, and he hoped it still fitted.

'All right. I'll send you the names of a few good tailors, just in case.'

Alex's computer dinged again and Sonya swiped her finger across her screen, in clear indication that she'd ticked that particular item off her list.

'I'm very pleased with the website—are you getting anything via the enquiries page?'

'Yes, quite a few things. Sofia's coordinating that.'

'Good. She seems very efficient. And the mural for your reception area? There are lots of possibilities there. How ever did you find these people? I've had a look at their previous work and it's stunning. Inspirational, even.'

'That was Marie's idea.'

'Of course…' Sonya's questioning gaze swept towards Marie.

'Oh. Yes, well… They're a group of artists who do wall art for charities and public spaces like hospitals and libraries. They choose the organisations they want to be involved with and work for free—we just pay for their materials.'

'And who's in charge?' Sonya enquired.

'Corinne Riley's their coordinator. She's about as much in charge as anyone is. She's an artist, and works part-time as an art therapist. Her husband, Tom, is head of Paediatrics at the hospital where I used to work.'

'And would they consider a magazine article, or even a short TV piece featuring their work here?'

Marie shrugged. 'I could ask. I know Corinne's very interested in spreading the word about how art can change spaces and involve people.'

'It's fascinating...' Sonya's mind was obviously hard at work on the possibilities. 'Yes, please. And I'd love an introduction if you feel that's appropriate?'

Alex smirked, wondering if Marie was taking notice of the fact that Sonya had just asked her for an introduction. It seemed she was, because she smiled suddenly.

'I'll email Corinne today and get back to you. Do you have any particular time in mind?'

'If she sends me a couple of dates which suit her I'll fit in with them.'

Sonya swiped again, and Alex braced himself for the next item on her agenda.

'You do have a suit, don't you?'

Now that Sonya had left, Alex's office seemed

a little quiet. Marie had waited to ask the awkward question.

'Somewhere. Unless I left it at the dry cleaner's...'

Marie frowned at him. 'It's not that suit you bought for your job interviews, is it?'

'What's wrong with that one?'

'It's not going to fit you any more.'

Alex put his hand on his stomach, sucking it in, and Marie laughed.

'I meant across the shoulders. You've lost those few extra pounds you were carrying.'

So she'd noticed. Alex couldn't help smirking. 'You think I've lost a bit of weight?'

She made a thing of eying him up and down. She was teasing, but her gaze made his stomach tighten with apprehension. When she grinned, it felt as if a warm wave was washing over him.

'You're in good shape, Alex. But you'll probably need a proper suit for these functions that Sonya was talking about.'

Alex sighed. 'Yes. Probably.'

'How many suits did you have when you were a child?' Marie homed in unerringly on the exact reason why Alex never wore a suit.

'Oh, about a dozen, all told. New ones each year.'

'That sounds excruciating.'

'It was.'

But he was doing things on his own terms now. Marie had told him that, and she wasn't going to underestimate him by reminding him again. In the silence he could feel her presence pushing the memories back and turning his gaze forward.

'You're right. I'll order two new suits; that old one probably doesn't fit me any more.'

She nodded. 'You'll be your own kind of excellent and glorious. What about some striped socks to match?'

Alex chuckled. His father would have blown a gasket at the thought of his wearing striped socks with a suit. Or with anything else, for that matter. Having to be excellent and glorious suddenly didn't seem so bad.

'Okay. Striped socks it is. You can choose them.'

The clinic's first week was reassuringly busy. Marie and Alex had agreed on a 'walking around' approach, to see how things were going and to iron out any teething problems, and they took turns with it. One dealt with patients and any urgent paperwork, and the other simply walked around the clinic, visiting all the different departments and talking to people.

It was working well—the staff were encouraged to talk about any difficulties they had, and the clinic's clients were beginning to know that either Marie or Alex would always be somewhere in the building if they wanted to chat.

'Hi, Terri. How are things going?' Marie saw a young mother with whom Alex had been working approaching her.

Terri's older child had been born with spina bifida, and although surgery had closed the opening in her spine, the little girl had been left with weakness in her legs and needed a specialist exercise regime.

'Good, thanks. This place is an absolute godsend.' Terri beamed at her. 'All that travelling we used to do to get to a hydrotherapy pool for Amy, and now we can just walk around the corner.'

'You're enjoying your swimming?' Marie grinned down at Terri's eight-year-old daughter and Amy nodded.

'*I'm* going to swim too.' Five-year-old Sam had been walking next to his sister's wheelchair, hanging obediently onto the side of it. 'I'm going to be a really good swimmer, and then I can help Amy.'

Terri grinned. 'It's great for both of them. We couldn't afford the time to take Sam to a class as well, but the hydrotherapist says she'll book Amy's sessions at the same time as the junior swim class, so Sam can swim too. Usually he just has to sit with me by the pool.'

'That's great.'

It was exactly what the clinic was for. Helping whole families to cope. Terri was looking less tired than she had when Marie had first met her.

'What's that?' Sam had left his sister's side and was standing on his toes, peering through the window into the courtyard.

'It's our garden. If you've got time, you can come and have a look.'

Marie shot a questioning look at Terri and she nodded. Opening the door, Marie let Sam into the courtyard and he started to run around, stopping in front of each planter to look at the flowers.

Terri parked Amy's wheelchair next to the water feature, so she could reach out to touch the plants around it. Then she sank down onto a nearby bench.

'This is lovely. I could stay here all day.'

Sam and Amy were amusing each other, and Terri gave a satisfied smile.

'Hello, Amy.' A woman stopped in the corridor by the open door. 'How are you, dear?'

'Very well, thank you, Miss Fletcher.' Amy sat a little straighter in her wheelchair and Marie suppressed a smile.

Jennifer Fletcher had been one of the first people through the doors when the clinic had opened. A retired primary school teacher, she seemed to know every child in the district, and had taught a number of their parents as well.

'This is lovely.' Jennifer craned her neck to see the garden, obviously hesitant to inspect it more closely without being asked.

'Come and join us, Miss Fletcher.' Terri grinned at her.

'It's about time you called me Jennifer.'

Miss Fletcher walked slowly across to the bench and Marie moved to make room for her.

'What brings you here…um… Jennifer?' Terri was clearly reticent about calling her old schoolteacher by her first name.

'I've been having a few aches and pains since I retired last spring, so I decided to come along and see if I could join an exercise class. I had a full physical, and the doctors have found I have an inflammation in my right hip.'

Jennifer beamed at Marie. She'd had the distinction of being the first patient to try out the new MRI scanner, and it had shown that, instead of a touch of arthritis, the bursa in her right hip was inflamed. Jennifer had professed delight at the thought that this could be rectified, and was already seeing the clinic's physiotherapist.

'I've got a full exercise programme and I think I'm doing rather well. It's early days, of course, but the physiotherapist here says that core strength is important as you enter your seventies.' Jennifer looked around the garden. 'You'll be adding a few bedding plants?'

'It's a work in progress. We've planted some seeds, and we have some cuttings over there in the corner.' Marie pointed to the yoghurt pots, full of water, where the cuttings were beginning to grow roots.

She saw Amy's head turn, and the little girl leaned over to see. 'I don't suppose you'd like to help us plant some, would you, Amy?'

'Mum...?' Amy turned to Terri.

'Of course. But we mustn't take up Dr Davies's time.' Terri flashed Marie an apologetic look.

'That's all right. If Amy would like to help with the garden—'

'Well, I would, too...' Jennifer spoke up.

It seemed that the garden had just acquired its first few volunteers.

Marie brought some of the pots over, moving a table so that Jennifer and Amy could work together, planting the Busy Lizzies. Sam had taken a couple of action figures from his mother's handbag, and he was playing with them.

'Would you like a drink? I'll pop over to the café.'

Everyone else was occupied and Terri deserved a break.

'You know what...?' Terri gave her a wry smile. 'I'd like to just stroll over there and get something. On my own. If you or Jennifer don't mind staying here with the kids, that is...?'

Marie knew the feeling well. Terri craved a moment to herself, so she could do something ordinary. She'd felt like that when she was a teenager. Wanting just five minutes that she could call her own, without one or other of her brothers wanting something.

'Of course. We'll be another half an hour with this, if you want to sit in the café?'

'No, that's okay. Can I get you something?' Terri pulled her purse out of her bag. 'My treat.'

If Marie wanted coffee, she had the lovely machine in her office. But that wasn't the point. It was clearly important to Terri that she get it, and she should accept the offer.

'A cup of tea would be nice. Thank you.'

Terri grinned, turning to Jennifer. 'Would you like a drink?'

Fifteen minutes later she saw Terri strolling back towards them, chatting to Alex. He was carrying a tray with four cups and a couple of child-sized boxes of juice, and when he'd handed the drinks around and stopped to find out how Jennifer and Amy were he strolled over to Sam to deliver his drink.

'They never quite grow up, do they?' Terri was drinking her coffee, watching Alex and Sam. The little boy had shown Alex his action figures, and the two were now busily engaged in making them jump from one planter to another. Sam jumped his onto the water feature with a splash and Alex followed with his, and the two figures started to fight in the swirling water.

By the time Terri said that they should go home, Alex's shirt was dappled with water. The pots were gathered up and labelled as Amy's, so that she could watch her plants grow and transfer them to the planters when they were big enough. Sam said goodbye to Alex, promising that they would continue their fight the next time he was here, and Alex thanked him gravely.

'I'm hoping your mother wouldn't have minded too much…' Marie nodded towards the water feature.

'Mind? She'd have loved it.' Alex grinned at her, coming to sit down on the bench.

'Good. And of course all that splashing about was entirely for Sam's benefit?'

It had occurred to Marie that Alex's love of silly games was because he'd never got the chance to play them when he was a child.

'Of course.' Alex brushed at his shirt, as if he'd only just noticed the water. 'I have absolutely no idea why you should think otherwise. Ooh—I had a call from Sonya.'

'What does she want us to do now?'

Sonya's calls generally meant smiling for one camera or another, but every time they did it Sofia Costa received a fresh wave of enquiries.

'It's an evening do at the Institute of Business. They throw a very select party once in a while, so their members can meet people who are doing groundbreaking work in various charitable and medical fields. Most big businesses like to have their names associated with a few good causes, and making those contacts now will help us in the future.'

Even the scale of Alex's wealth wasn't going to finance his dreams of creating and running a chain of clinics all over the country. This was about the future—one that Alex was going to build for himself.

'That sounds great. Does Sonya know someone at the Institute?'

'No, but it turns out that a couple of the Institute's board of directors went to my school and they vaguely remember me. Sonya's managed to swing a couple of invitations.'

'So Sonya's going with you?' That would be good. She'd keep Alex in line and on message.

'No, she's going with her husband. The second invitation is for you.'

'What?' All the quiet peace of the garden suddenly evaporated. 'Tell me you're joking, Alex.'

'Why would I be? You have as much to say about the clinic as me.'

He leaned forward, his eyes betraying the

touch of mischief that Marie loved so much. At any other time than this.

'And the whole point of a man's dinner suit is to show off a woman's dress.'

Suddenly she felt sick. 'I can't hobnob with the rich and famous, Alex. I don't know how to talk with these people, or how to act.'

'How about just the same as you always do?'

There was a trace of hurt in his voice. *He* was rich. And it was only a matter of time before he'd be famous. She knew Alex was under no illusions that he could keep his royal status under wraps indefinitely—he just wanted to put the moment off for as long as he could.

'I can't, Alex. I just…can't.'

He thought for a moment, his face grave. 'Okay. If you can't do it, then you can't. I'm not going to tell you that the clinic needs you, or that I need you, because that wouldn't give you any choice. You're always there for the people who need you.'

'What do you mean?' The lump in Marie's throat betrayed her. She knew exactly what he meant.

'You've always been there for your mother and brothers. Don't get me wrong—that's a fine thing, and I envy you it. I'd have done anything for my mother to need me a bit more. But I know it's not been easy for you; it never is for people who care for the people they love.'

She'd been thinking the same about Terri, just moments ago. He was right, but Marie dismissed the thought. It was too awkward.

'So you're telling me I don't have to go?'

'Of course. You don't *have* to do anything. I'd really like you to go, because I think you're selling yourself short. And because a very wise person once told me that I needed to accept who I am and write my own script. I'd like you to accept who I am and come with me, as my friend.'

Dammit. Saying he needed her would have been easy compared to this. Alex was reaching out, asking her to step out of her comfort zone and meet him halfway.

'So when is this reception?'

'Next month. I could go dress-shopping with you…?'

He looked as if he'd enjoy that far too much.

'No, that's fine. I can handle that.'

'Then you're coming?'

'Yes, all right. I'll come.'

At least it would serve as a reminder to her that she and Alex came from different worlds. That they could be friends, but anything more was unthinkable. It had always been unthinkable, but it was doubly so now that they were working together.

He grinned. 'Great. I'll let Sonya know. Should I quit while I'm winning?'

She could never resist his smile. 'Yes. Please do that, Alex.'

CHAPTER SEVEN

MARIE HAD BOUGHT Alex an action figure. She reckoned it was what every boy needed, in case someone turned up in his office needing to play, and Alex had arranged the jointed arms and legs so that the figure leant nonchalantly against one of the plant pots on his windowsill.

She tried to repress a yawn, failing miserably. Jennifer Fletcher had expressed enthusiasm over an idea for a carers' support group for mums like Terri, and said that she had another couple of friends who might be interested in helping. They were having to sort out all the relevant statutory checks for the volunteers who were going to be working with children, and assess the needs of the kids so that the clinic could provide the professional staff that would be required. It was going to take a couple of hours.

'Why don't we finish for the evening? This can wait,' said Alex.

'It can't, Alex. We've both got a full day tomorrow.'

And Marie had left work at five o'clock sharp for the last couple of evenings. She was feeling guilty about having left Alex alone working, but her mother was having one of her crises and Marie had been up late, talking her down.

He opened his mouth, obviously about to protest, but the sound of the front gates rattling silenced him.

Alex went to the window, and then turned. 'Nisha's outside. You don't have an appointment with her, do you?'

'No, all her medical tests came back okay, so I referred her to our relationship counsellor…'

Marie followed Alex outside and saw that Nisha was walking away from the gates now. He hurried to unlock them.

'I'm sorry…' Nisha turned back to him, tears streaming down her face. 'I shouldn't have come…'

'That's all right. Come inside and tell us what the matter is.'

Alex's question provoked more tears. 'When I spoke to Anita at the clinic she said that we didn't have to have sex…we could just spend time together. But one thing led to another…'

It was a measure of her distress that Nisha had forgotten all her reticence in talking about the problem.

'Okay, well, come inside.'

Alex glanced at Marie. He had no hesitation in talking to patients about sexual matters, but he was clearly wondering if Nisha wouldn't feel more comfortable discussing this with Marie.

'We had such a lovely time. But now it hurts to pee, and I'm passing blood. Carol says it's cystitis. What am I going to tell my husband?'

Alex frowned, clearly wondering whether Nisha wanted him to respond or not.

Marie decided to put him out of his misery. 'Let's go inside, eh? Alex, why don't you take the pushchair?'

'I'm so sorry. It's later than I thought—you must be closed by now...'

'That's okay. I'm glad you came.'

That was almost the truth. Marie *was* glad Nisha had asked for help—she just wished she'd needed it on another evening, when she wasn't so tired. But when she took Nisha's hand she felt it warm and trembling in hers and forgot all about that.

Nisha was running a fever, and clearly not at all well. After Marie had tested a sample of her urine, to confirm Carol's diagnosis, she curled up on the examination couch, shivering and crying.

'Can we call your husband? I think it would be best if he came and picked you up.'

Nisha nodded. 'I'm so disappointed. I thought we were doing everything right, at last...'

'I know it's easy to feel it is, but this is not your fault. Recovery isn't always a straight line; it's sometimes two steps forward and one step back. But this is an infection and we can deal with it. You'll feel a lot better when the antibiotics start to take effect.'

'Sorry...'

Marie smiled at Nisha. 'And stop apologising, will you? This is what we're here for.'

'I'm so glad you *are* here. Thank you.'

Nisha's husband arrived—a quiet, smiling man, who made sure that the first thing he did was hug his wife.

Prompted by Marie, Nisha told him what had happened and he nodded. 'I'll stay home from work tomorrow to look after you.'

'No. You don't need to...'

But Nisha obviously wanted him to, and Marie guessed it wouldn't take much before she gave in and accepted his offer.

'Give us a call if there's anything we can help with.' She handed Nisha's husband her card. 'If the clinic's closed, you can use the out-of-hours number; there will be someone on hand to advise you.'

'Thank you—for everything. I'll take good care of her.' Nisha's husband helped her down from the couch, putting his arm around her protectively.

Alex opened the gates and bade the couple goodbye, reserving a special smile for the child in the pushchair, who had slept soundly through the whole thing.

Then he turned, walking back to his office, where Marie was waiting for him. He picked up her laptop and papers, tucking them under his arm. 'We're going back to mine. We'll get a take-away.'

Just like the old days. When he'd brook none of her arguments about needing to work and insist she take a break for just one evening. That had usually involved food, as well, and the tradition had persisted. His flat was on her way home, and after a day spent at the clinic it would be nice to talk over a meal.

'It's my turn to get the takeaway, isn't it? Shall we go for Thai this time?' Marie's resources stretched to taking her turn in paying for the food now.

He shrugged, picking up his car keys. 'That sounds great.'

Alex's flat was on the top floor of a mansion block in Hampstead. Quiet and secluded, but just moments away from a parade of artisan food shops and cafés, and little boutiques that sold clothes with hefty price tags.

Inside, it reeked of quiet quality. Large rooms with high ceilings, and a hallway that was built to accommodate cupboards and storage and still give more than enough space. Alex might have rejected his father's lifestyle, but he'd absorbed an appreciation for nice things, and he always bought the best he could afford. The sofas were the same ones he'd had in medical school, but they were still as comfortable and looked as good. If you could afford it, there was economy in that.

'You order. I'll put some music on. What do you fancy? A little late-night jazz?'

The sitting room was lined with cabinets that housed Alex's extensive books and music collection. Marie had never hesitated in sharing his music with him—it was one of those things that cost nothing and brought them both joy.

But it wasn't late-night yet, even though Marie felt tired enough. 'Late-night jazz is going to send me to sleep.'

'Right. Driving music?'

'No, that's a bit too wakey-uppy. Have you got a soul mix?'

It was a rhetorical question. Alex chuckled. There was a pause while he decided which soul mix fitted the occasion best, and then a muted beat began to fill the room.

They began to work, spreading their papers out on the large glass-topped coffee table. When the food came they added a couple of plates and a jumble of takeaway cartons. Ideas came more easily in this setting, and by the time they were ready for coffee they were finished.

He stood, stretching his limbs with satisfaction. Marie leant forward to gather up the plates and he batted her hand away.

'Leave it, will you? Try relaxing for a few minutes.'

It was impossible not to, in the heat of his smile and the rhythm of the music.

'I'll take a hot towel for my face while you're there...' she called after him as he made his way to the kitchen, laden down with the remnants of their meal.

'Sorry, ma'am, we're fresh out of hot towels. Coffee will have to do.'

Marie rolled her eyes, teasing him. 'No hot towels? What kind of service is this? I'm not coming back here again!'

'I've got a dark roast arabica...' he shouted through from the kitchen, and Marie chuckled. Alex always served good coffee.

'You're almost forgiven,' she shouted back.

He returned with two cups of black coffee, with a thick foamy crema on top. Even the smell of it was gorgeous.

'That's it. This is definitely a five-star establishment.'

'It can't possibly be. I'm not done yet.' He

grinned at her, catching her hand. 'I've got moves.'

Another one of those old jokes that had stood the test of time. They both loved to dance, and Alex's grinning query as to whether *she* had moves, and his promise that he had a few of his own, would often prompt them to dance until they were exhausted. Marie had often wondered whether it was a substitute for sex, but had decided not to think too deeply on the question.

'My moves are already asleep. I will be too, as soon as I get home.'

Alex was far too tempting at the moment. Too delicious and complicated. She'd never wanted to be one of those women who went out with Alex for a few months only to see him walk away without looking back.

'Are you sure? You're tapping your foot.'

He turned the music up, trying to tempt her, but when Marie laughed and shook her head, he turned it back down again.

'Okay, your loss. It means you'll just have to tell me what the matter is.'

'Nothing. I'm just tired…'

How many times had Alex heard Marie say that nothing was the matter? How many times had he asked and felt shut out when she wouldn't talk about it? He'd accepted it once, but it was becoming more and more difficult to take what she said at face value and turn away from her.

'I can wait you out.' He sat down, taking a sip of his coffee.

Marie smiled. How she managed to do that, when she was so tired she could hardly keep her eyes open and clearly worried about something, was beyond him.

'Great coffee.'

'Yes, it's a good blend.' Alex decided that Marie's diversionary tactics weren't going to work on him any more. 'I'm still waiting.'

She puffed out a breath. 'It's nothing, really. I just... I was up a bit late last night, talking to my mum. She's worried about my youngest brother.'

'What about you? Are you worried about him?'

She gave a frustrated shrug. 'I'm *always* worried about Zack.'

This was something new. Alex knew Marie had always supported her younger brothers, but she'd never really said much about the day-to-day process of that. Just that her mum often found that three boys could be hard to handle on her own and needed a bit of help. Alex had assumed that Marie helped out financially, but it seemed there was more to it than that.

'What's the problem?'

Perhaps he'd remind her that they'd been friends for a long time. Maybe he'd even mention that Marie had given him a hard time over the secrets he'd kept.

'You know… He's twenty…'

'He's having difficulty finding time to study and check out all the bands he needs to see?'

She laughed suddenly. 'No, Alex. He's not like *you* when you were twenty. Anyway, you never seemed to have much difficulty keeping up.'

'Yeah. It was easy. You managed your studies, as many jobs as you could find, *and* about five minutes per day for recreation. So what's Zack not managing to do?'

She shrugged, reaching for her coffee cup. That was a sure signal that she was done talking.

They'd been through a lot together over the years. Studying, dancing, working until they were too tired even to speak. He'd carried her into her bedroom once and then turned his back, walking away, because the one thing Alex had always known for sure was that he couldn't take things any further with Marie.

He'd rejected the idea that he'd always loved her and instead he'd asked her to help him build a clinic. But he *had* always loved her, and when she turned her gaze on him, her eyes dark in the approaching dusk, he knew he wasn't going to flinch from this.

'What is Zack not managing to do?' he repeated. He heard the quiet demand in his tone and saw surprise on Marie's face.

For a moment he thought she would get up and leave, but then she spoke.

'At the moment he's not managing to do anything very much. He did well with his A levels, but decided he wanted to take a year out before university. I think it was just that he couldn't get motivated to choose a course. I got all the prospectuses and sat down with him, but he wasn't very enthusiastic about it.'

'So he's working?'

'No. He had a few jobs, but couldn't stick at any of them. He's been unemployed for the last six months, and increasingly he's staying up all night and sleeping all day. Mum doesn't know what to do with him. A few days ago he took money from her purse and went out. He came back the following afternoon, went straight upstairs and slept for fourteen hours. She's worried he might have been taking drugs, but I took a look at him and didn't see any signs of it.'

'How much money did he take?' Alex felt a cold weight settle in his chest. This wasn't fair…

'Two hundred pounds. She'd just gone to the bank to get the money for her main monthly food shop. She can't afford that; she's already keeping him in food and clothes.'

'So you gave her the money?'

Marie rolled her eyes. 'What else was I supposed to do? I told Zack this was absolutely the last time, and that I wasn't going to bale him out again.'

'Did he listen?'

'Yes, he listened. Listening's not the problem with Zack. He'll hear what you have to say, and tell you all the things he thinks you want to hear. Then he'll ignore it all and do exactly as he likes. Mum knows he's got to change, but she makes excuses for him. About how he's never had a strong father figure, and how she's not been able to give him enough time because she's at work.'

The words came out in a rush of frustration. Then Marie reddened a little, as if she'd made a faux pas by admitting that there was something she couldn't manage on her own. He wasn't going to give up on her now.

'What about your other brothers?' He knew that both of Marie's other brothers had been to university and had good jobs.

'Dan's washed his hands of him completely—he says Zack needs to pull himself together. And Pete lives up in Sunderland. He tried talking to him last time he was down on a visit, but Zack just gave him that lovely smile of his and told him everything will work out.'

'And your mother?'

'She's...she does her best. Mum's fragile. She

had a breakdown when my dad left, and we were all put into foster homes for a while. It was awful.'

Alex nodded. Marie had told him, years ago, how all she'd wanted when she was a kid was to have her family back together and to keep it that way. At the time he'd almost envied her for having something she cared about so much.

'It never was your fault, Marie. You didn't have to be the one to put things right.'

A single tear rolled down her cheek. Suddenly the room was far too big and the distance between them too great. He couldn't reach for her and comfort her, and if he moved she'd only shoo him away and tell him that she was okay.

'In a way, it was my fault. My dad left because a wife and four children was too much for him. He couldn't deal with it. My mum broke down over it…'

'You were ten years old.' The impulse to hold her and comfort her was wearing him down fast. 'You were trying to clear up a mess that adults had made.'

'Families, huh? Who'd have them?' She brushed away the tears and gave him a smile.

Was he supposed to empathise with that? Alex reckoned so. And Marie was only telling him what he already knew. He couldn't contemplate having a family of his own because he'd lived with the consequences of failure and seen what they had done to his mother. Marie had lived with the consequences of failure as well, and she needed someone who would be there for her.

Maybe that was why he'd always maintained his distance. He'd helped her as much as she would let him in practical terms, but always shied away from the emotional. It was time to redraw the boundaries.

'What do you need?'

She shrugged, shaking her head. 'I've had a takeaway and some music. Now an early night.'

She obviously wasn't going to discuss the matter any further, and Alex needed a plan. Something with no loose ends, that she wouldn't be able to argue with or reject out of hand. Something that was going to work and maybe change things in the long term.

'I'll take you home, then.'

'That's okay. It's early enough to take the Tube.'

Alex got to his feet. 'You can take the Tube, then, and I'll drive over to your place. I'll see you there.'

The expected smile almost tore his heart in two.

'Since you're going my way, I suppose I *could* ask you to drop me off, then.'

He walked through into the hall, picking up his car keys and waiting for her there. Marie appeared, her bag slung across her shoulder, but before he could reach for the latch on the front door she suddenly flung her arms around his waist.

'Uh!' He allowed his hands to move slowly towards her back, returning her hug as impersonally as he could. 'What was that for?'

'For being my best friend. And for listening to me blather on.'

She hugged him tight, and then let him go, stepping back. Alex's knees almost gave way.

'This is just between you and me, right?'

She saw everyone else's needs and yet treated her own as weakness. And she was clearly regretting saying as much as she had.

'Of course. What are friends for?'

The look on her face seemed a lot like relief that he'd decided to drop the subject. For once, Marie had misread him. Alex wasn't going to back off and if she put up a fight then so be it.

He'd fight her back.

A good night's sleep had applied some perspective to the matter. Marie would deal with Zack, and she'd deal with her mum the way she always had. Alex couldn't help her with this.

She retreated to her office, and then spent most of the day showing a few local GPs and hospital doctors around the clinic while Alex saw patients. Working together with other health professionals, becoming one of their options when they thought about what their patients needed, was a must if the clinic was going to reach its full potential for helping the community.

When Alex appeared in the doorway she couldn't help starting. Last night had lit a slow-burning fuse, which had been fizzling all day. Sometimes it seemed to go out, but that was just an illusion. The spark never quite died.

'How was your day?'

His question was much the same as it usually was when they'd been working on separate things and hadn't seen much of each other.

'Good, thanks. They all seemed impressed with what we had to offer, and a couple of them have said that they already have patients on their books they'd like to refer.'

'That sounds great.'

He dipped his hand into his pocket and put a small box on her desk. Marie looked inside, finding a tangle of pink paper clips, and when she tipped some of them out she saw that they were in different animal shapes.

'They're wonderful—thank you. Where do you get all this crazy stuff?' Marie already had a collection of unusually shaped, brightly coloured things on her desk, which Alex had bought for her.

'That's my secret. If you knew, you wouldn't

need me to feed your stationery habit. And, by the way, I saw Anita just now. She popped in to see Nisha today.'

'Yes? How is she?'

Alex had clearly decided to forget her show of emotion last night, and they were back to business as usual. If he could do it, then so could she.

'Feeling much better.' He grinned. 'I'm going to stick with that blanket assurance and leave the details to you and Anita. I imagine that Nisha will be more comfortable with that.'

'Good move.'

Marie bit her tongue. She didn't need to be thinking about Alex's moves—or hers. Last night was last night.

Alex seemed to be loitering, neither sitting down to talk nor about to leave. Suddenly he planted his hands on her desk, leaning forward towards her.

'I want Zack.'

'You…want Zack?'

Marie felt her jaw harden. Alex obviously thought he could solve this problem, but he didn't know Zack.

'What for? There's nothing you can do, Alex.'

'Why on earth not? We're friends, Marie. Heaven forbid we'd actually try to help each other with our problems.'

All right. He had her there.

'I can deal with it. I appreciate the offer, but—'

'It's not an offer. You can't deal with this on your own, and I can help. You told me I had to accept what I've been given and do the right thing with it. I'm just following your advice.'

'Well…what are you going to do with him?'

Alex was clearly on a mission. If she wasn't so cross with her brother for treating their mum so badly Marie might have felt sorry for Zack.

Alex straightened up. He suddenly seemed very tall, his determination filling the room. 'He's going to work here. I've had a word with Sofia, and there are a lot of things she can get him to do, so he'll be working hard. He'll need to, because he's going to have to pay you back the two hundred pounds he took.'

'That doesn't matter, Alex. It's done now.'

'It matters. This isn't about the money. It's about how he treats people. I need you to take the two hundred pounds and for your mother to accept something from him for his bed and board. Everything else I'll deal with. He'll work a full day and he'll pull his weight. If he turns up here with a hangover I'll find a job for him that'll make a cracking headache even worse. And if I see any evidence of drug-taking I'll test him myself and put him into our drug rehab programme.'

It was exactly what Zack needed. But Alex shouldn't have to do this.

'The clinic can't afford it, Alex. We have budgets and that money could be spent elsewhere.'

'Yes, but it appears that I have a small inheritance on my hands, and my income is embarrassing enough to be able to pay Zack without even noticing the difference. My real problem is *you*. Which I guess makes you Zack's real problem as well.'

Marie felt herself redden. Alex was right— she was standing between Zack and an amazing opportunity.

'He does need something like this. Zack's just so charming that he thinks that everyone will forgive him anything. He's right, and I'm just as much at fault as anyone in falling for his promises...'

Alex chuckled, finally sitting down. '*I* can be charming, can't I? You never have any problem resisting that.'

'That's different. I respect you.'

'Okay. I'm not sure how that works, but I'll take it. Can you get your mother on board?' Alex finally sat down.

'Yes. That won't be a problem.'

Alex had come up with a plan that would make a real difference for Zack. Marie had to acknowledge that with good grace.

'Thank you, Alex. It would do him a lot of good, and I really appreciate your help. If you're willing to take him on for a couple of weeks, that would be great.'

He smiled. If he was about to make some comment about how that hadn't been so difficult to agree to, then she was going to throw him out of her office.

'I want him for more than a couple of weeks. I reckon it'll take him a little while to earn enough to pay you, and he's going to have to do all the boring jobs that no one else wants. When he's earned it, he'll get the chance to choose something that interests him. I'll be reviewing things with him every month, and if he decides on a study path then we'll support him in that. If he wants to look for employment then he'll get the experience he needs, and I'll write him a great reference.'

'This is too much, Alex.' Marie couldn't think of a reason why it was too much, just knew that it was.

'That's what I'm offering. Take it or leave it, Marie. But know this—I'll think less of you if you turn down an opportunity for Zack just because of your own pride.'

She felt herself redden. Alex had just stripped her of all her excuses, and the loss of that armour made her want to shiver. If it had been anyone else she wouldn't have been able to countenance it.

'I'll take it. Thank you, Alex.'

'It's my pleasure. Is tomorrow too early for an interview? Or do you need a bit more time to convince your mother and Zack?'

'Tomorrow's great.' Marie frowned. 'He won't be wearing a suit, though…'

Alex chuckled. 'Good—neither will I. Will nine o'clock suit him?'

'He'll be there.'

'Right, then.' Alex looked at his watch. 'It's nearly five o'clock now and I guess you'll be needing to go.'

It would have been nice to stay a little longer. Zack was difficult to contend with at the moment, and Marie wanted Alex's company. She loved the give and take that had developed between them, which made her feel that it was possible to step into new territory.

But she did need to speak to her mother, and to Zack. If he was going to make the best of this opportunity she needed to prepare him, convince him that this was an opportunity and not a punishment.

'Yes, thanks. I'll…um…see you tomorrow, then. With Zack.'

'You will.' He got to his feet, a satisfied smile on his face. 'You're doing the right thing, Marie.'

'Yes, I know…'

She wanted to hug him again. For caring and

for being the tower of strength that had given her a way to really help her brother. Alex had been a true friend.

'You were right. Thank you.'

He narrowed his eyes. 'I think we'll never mention that again.'

Alex's dry humour always made her laugh. 'Yes, okay. It'll be our secret.'

CHAPTER EIGHT

Marie had done her part. She'd convinced her mother that this was exactly what Zack needed, and then the two of them had hauled him out of his room and given him little choice but to accept the plan. Zack, as always, had been accommodating and cheerful at the prospect of working for his keep and paying back the money he'd taken. Whether he would stick with it for more than a week would be the real test.

She'd called round to her mother's house at seven-thirty the next morning and found Zack sorting through shirts, throwing them onto the bed. Marie gathered them up, putting them back onto their hangers.

'Mum's ironed all these.'

Sometimes she felt like a broken record, nagging Zack about everything. Like the grumpy big sister who squeezed all the joy out of his life.

'Sorry, sis.' Zack gave her a winning smile. 'I just want to make a good impression. I don't want to let you down.'

'I'm not your problem.' Zack knew she loved

him, even though he did make her want to scream at times. 'This is about not letting yourself down.'

'Okay...' Zack frowned at the line of shirts that Marie had put back into the wardrobe and then whipped out a checked shirt with a plain tie that matched one of the colours. 'What about this?'

'Perfect. My handsome little brother.'

'I don't want to look handsome. I want to look...contrite. Hard-working. That kind of thing.' He pulled a face that indicated deep sorrow.

Marie rolled her eyes. 'Don't pull that one with me, Zack. I'm not Mum. You're going to look nice because this is an interview, but just turning up and saying the right things isn't going to get you off the hook. Afterwards is when you get to prove whether or not you're contrite and hard-working.'

She got yet another of Zack's dazzling smiles. That was his trouble; he never took anything too seriously. She was going to have to keep a close watch on him if he came to work at the clinic.

'All right. Half an hour to get washed and dressed and have a shave. Then we're leaving.'

Getting Zack to the clinic was a bit like getting a recalcitrant six-year-old to school. But at least he straightened up a bit and smiled cheerfully when Alex came out of his office and greeted him.

Alex whisked Zack and Sofia into his office, shutting the door firmly behind them. It wouldn't do to listen at the door, so Marie returned to her office and frowned at the wall, fiddling with a pink paper clip.

After an hour, she called down to Reception, asking Tina to give her a buzz as soon as Alex was free. Zack might be blissfully free from interview nerves, but Marie couldn't help worrying about him.

Zack was a graceful, engaging youth, with a ready smile. He declared himself ready for all kinds of hard work, and was excited at the prospect of earning the opportunities that Alex and Sofia outlined. Yes, he wanted to study. And, yes, he wanted to take responsibility for all the jobs in the clinic that no one else wanted to do. He wanted to show that he could take on the outreach tasks that Sonya had outlined as well. But if he could manage to do all that, he'd be working for more hours than Marie had at his age, and that wasn't really possible.

Despite himself, Alex liked the kid. He was charming and intelligent and he reminded him of Marie. And there was something in those heavy-lashed blue eyes that made Alex feel the boy might just have the same grit as his sister, if it were only possible to bring it out in him.

After they'd shown Zack around Alex left him in Sofia's care. Then he returned to his office and waited.

He didn't have to wait long. Marie appeared in the doorway, clearly trying to give the impression that she'd just happened to walk past on her way somewhere else. She put a large piece of card face down on his desk and sat down. They'd fallen into the habit of bringing things for each other's offices—unusual stationery or pictures for the walls—and he turned the card over, wondering what she'd found this time.

'Oh! That's wonderful. Where shall I put it?'

His wall was filling up now, and he'd brought some pictures and vintage record covers from home to go with the various prints Marie had given him. This one was an old photograph she'd got from somewhere, which reeked of late nights and the blues, showing a drink propped on top of a piano and one of his favourite artists, shirt-sleeves rolled up and eyes closed as he played.

'You're beginning to run out of space.' Marie surveyed the wall.

'Not for this one.'

It was clearly something Marie had gone out of her way to get, and an image that Alex hadn't seen before. He took one of the framed pictures off its hook, and started to prise open the back of it, so he could replace it with the photograph and put it in pride of place.

Marie obviously wasn't going to ask, so he told her anyway. 'Zack seems…unrealistically enthusiastic.'

Marie laughed. 'Yes, that's him all over.'

'Maybe an eight-hour day will slake his zeal a little.'

'He'll be here before nine o'clock tomorrow morning. I promise.'

Marie flashed him that intent look that he'd seen so many times before. When she took on the troubles of the world and tried to work her way through them. She usually succeeded, but Alex had seen the toll it had taken.

'Will you do me a favour? Don't go round to your mother's every morning and chivvy him.'

'He told you about that?' Marie looked a little as if she'd been found out.

'No, I guessed. You have enough to do here, without running around after Zack.'

Alex could see that this wasn't reason enough for Marie and decided she needed a bit more persuasion.

'I've told him that he'll work eight hours, with an hour's lunch break every day. If he's late then he can work an extra hour in the evening, but he's not to stay here after six o'clock. If he gets here after ten in the morning I'll dock his pay.'

'That's very generous. He really should be here at nine every day.'

'Flexible hours work for us. But he needs to take responsibility for himself. I'm hoping your mother won't decide to give him spending money for the weekend if he finds his pay has been docked at the end of the week.'

Marie shook her head. 'No, she'll do whatever you ask; she's really grateful that you're taking Zack on. I'll mention it to her, though.'

She seemed a little unhappy with the arrangement, and Alex answered the question that she hadn't asked but which was clearly bothering her.

'You won't be helping him, Marie. Let him suffer the consequences if he can't get here on time. If he needs to be told to buck his ideas up, let Sofia and me do it.'

She saw the sense in it and nodded.

'I rather wish I had brothers or sisters.' Alex leaned back in his chair. It would have been nice to have someone to care about so ferociously. Someone for whom he'd do anything.

'Sometimes they're a pain in the neck.'

'You wouldn't be without them, though.'

'No. I wouldn't. Even Zack.'

She loved her little brother. He was driving her to distraction at the moment, but she loved him all the same. And she'd given him to Alex, trusting that he'd do the right thing. Alex felt a little unequal to the prospect, but it warmed him all the same.

'So…' All that was better left unsaid. 'Anything you want to discuss?'

'I've got the ideas for the mural in Reception back. Would you like to see them?'

'Not really.'

Marie's eyebrows shot up.

'Surprise me.'

She did that all the time, and it was always fantastic. Alex wondered vaguely what he'd do if Marie ever left the clinic. Left *him*.

But that wasn't going to happen. He wouldn't let it.

Alex had stayed out of the way while the artists took over the reception area. He had a final fitting for his dinner suit, and a few other errands to run, and although he'd spent most of the day itching to see what Marie was doing he'd decided that this was her project and she should be allowed to enjoy it alone.

Zack had expressed a fervent desire to come in on Saturday and help, and since he'd managed to turn up on time for nine of the last ten working days Sofia had allowed it.

When he'd arrived at two in the afternoon one day he'd been abject in his apologies. Alex had smilingly shrugged them off and simply docked his pay. After that, Zack had made sure he wasn't late again.

Alex arrived at the clinic at four o'clock and saw a dark-haired man walking across the courtyard, pushing a buggy and talking to the small boy who walked beside it. Alex caught him up. He introduced himself and they shook hands.

'I'm Tom Riley—Corinne's husband. That's Matthew, and this is Chloe...' He bent down to the pushchair, taking the little girl out of it and letting her stagger uncertainly towards her brother.

'We really appreciate this, Tom. I know your wife has a waiting list for this kind of thing.'

Tom chuckled. 'I get to spend a day with the kids, and Cori gets to cover herself with paint. What's not to like about that—particularly when it's for a project as exciting as this one? Although I'm still cross with you for poaching Marie away from the hospital.'

'I needed someone who's the best at what they do.'

Alex shot Tom an apologetic look and he laughed.

'Then you made the right choice. I'm interested to see what you're doing here; some of my patients' families live in this borough.' Tom swung round, calling to Matthew. 'Leave the tree alone,

CHAPTER NINE

LAST WEEK HAD been all about getting paint in his hair and under his fingernails. After work every day Alex had donned a pair of overalls and laboriously filled one of the walls in the children's playroom, using the stencils Cori had given them. Zack had been allowed to help too, on account of being on time each day, and doing every job that Sofia gave him cheerfully and well. He was showing real artistic flair, bringing life to Alex's rather flat representations with a just a few extra brushstrokes.

This weekend was entirely different. Alex had picked up his evening suit from the tailor and gone to the bank to open his safety deposit box. He'd scrubbed every trace of paint off under the shower, and while he towelled himself dry he regarded the suit that was hanging on the door of the wardrobe.

He sat down on the bed. He'd actually rather go naked tonight than pull that dark jacket on over a crisp white shirt. And the bow tie? He had a step-by-step diagram, downloaded from the internet, but he'd never tied a bow tie himself. His mother had always done that for him, brushing specks of dust from his jacket and telling him he looked every inch a prince.

Suddenly he missed her very much. Planting the flowers that spelt out her name and switching on the water feature in the garden had felt like his own very personal goodbye. It had awakened feelings that Alex had tried hard to repress.

Would his mother have loved the clinic the way he did, and allowed it to bring some colour into her life? Or would she have stubbornly clung to his father, fading into his shadow?

But thinking about that now would only make it harder to put the suit on, and there was no way he could answer the door to Marie in this state of undress. Alex pulled the white shirt across his shoulders, looking at the full-length mirror in the corner of the room as he did so. He'd lost all the extra weight he'd put on and felt better for it.

He picked up the pair of striped socks Marie had added to his ensemble and smiled. He was ready for anything now.

Almost anything.

When the doorbell rang he wasn't ready for Marie.

She smiled at him, stepping into the hallway. 'Where's your tie?'

'Uh?'

She was wearing a pair of high-heeled black

court shoes, which made her legs look even longer than usual. She had a dark green brocade coat
on, fitted at the waist, and her hair was sleek and
shining. She looked stunning.

'Alex!' She snapped her fingers in front of his
face. 'Earth to Alex!'

'Yes. Nearly ready.'

That was about all he could manage in the
way of communication at that moment. He just
wanted to drink her in.

She put a small black clutch bag down on the
hall table and started to unbutton her coat.

Where were his manners?

Alex helped her out of the coat, admiring the
shape of her arms and the silky softness of her
skin. The plain, sleeveless green dress was perfect, because it didn't draw any attention away
from her beauty. It was flattering, slim at the
waist to show the curve of her hips and breasts.

Alex decided not to think the word 'breasts'
again tonight; it would be sure to get him in trouble.

'Please tell me you didn't forget to get a tie.'
She was looking at him quizzically. 'I'm not sure
I can manage a late-night mercy dash to your tai-
lor in these heels.'

'I've got a tie. And some instructions.'

She turned the corner of her mouth down in a

look of resigned humour. 'You want me to give it a go?'

'Yes. Please.'

He went to retrieve the tie and found her sitting in the lounge, perched on the edge of a chair, her legs folded neatly in front of her. He was beginning to revise his opinion of formal dress.

'Let's give it a go, then.' She took the instructions from his hand and studied them carefully. 'I haven't done this before, but it doesn't look so difficult...'

She got to her feet again, reaching up to button his collar. The touch of her fingers against his neck made him feel a little dizzy.

Consulting the diagram every now and then, she went through each step carefully. She was concentrating too hard on getting the tie right to be as aware as he was of how close they were.

'That's okay.' He glanced at his reflection in the mirror over the fireplace. The tie was slightly crooked, but it was a big improvement on any of his efforts.

'No, it isn't—it's lopsided. Come here, I'll give it another go.'

Marie untied the bowtie and Alex stared at the ceiling, glad that he didn't have to look her in the eye. He could feel the brush of her body against his, and reminded himself yet again that breasts were a forbidden thought.

'I think that's it.' She stood back to survey her handiwork and gave a little nod. Alex looked in the mirror.

'That's perfect. Thanks.'

'Okay, now the jacket.'

They'd said they would stick together tonight, and Marie was making his dislike of dressing up much easier to bear. Alex fetched his jacket, and handed her the pocket handkerchief. She folded it carefully and brushed a speck of dust from his shoulder. Then she tucked the handkerchief into his top pocket and Alex buttoned his jacket.

'Let me look at you.' She stepped back for a moment, looking him up and down. 'That's great, Alex. You've scrubbed up *very* nicely.'

'You…' Alex realised suddenly that he hadn't told her how wonderful she looked, and that he really should make some effort to do her justice. 'You've scrubbed up really well too.'

It was a paltry kind of compliment, but Marie was still pleased with it. 'Are we ready to go, then?'

Not quite.

He went to his bedroom to fetch the velvet-covered box he'd taken from the bank that morning. 'I thought… I mean, I'd be very honoured if you would wear this.'

She stared at him. Maybe this hadn't been such a good idea after all. Alex knew Marie was nervous about tonight, and he'd reckoned this would maybe give her confidence. It was a bauble that would outshine anything that any of the society women might wear.

He'd committed himself now, though. He opened the box, taking out the exquisitely crafted platinum-and-gold chain, the delicate filigree strands of which were deceptively strong. They had to be, to support the large diamond that hung from it.

Marie backed away from him. 'That must be... That's... How big is it?'

'Um...around twenty carats, I think.' Thirty-one, actually.

'It's got to be worth an absolute fortune. Alex, I can't wear this. We're going to be asking people for money.'

'That's not really how it works. I couldn't sell the Crown Jewels to raise funds for the clinic even if I wanted to. They're held in trust.'

Marie shook her head, tears welling in her eyes. She blinked them away furiously, trying not to spoil her make-up, and Alex regretted his gesture immediately.

'Marie, I'm sorry...'

His apology seemed to upset her even more, and a tear rolled down her cheek, leaving a thin trail of mascara.

'You don't have to be sorry, Alex. I just... I can't wear this. It's too good for me.'

'Oh, no. I'm not having that. Nothing's too good for you, Marie.'

She sniffed and he handed her his handkerchief. She dabbed at her eyes, trying to smile.

'Alex, I really appreciate this; it's a generous and kind gesture. But I'm not someone who wears diamonds. I can't meet the people who are going to be there tonight on their terms, and you told me it was okay to meet them on mine.'

That was the crux of it all. Marie saw them as being stranded on opposite ends of a spectrum—so much so that she couldn't even accept the loan of a necklace for the evening. Maybe she was right. Maybe asking her to fit in with the kind of people he'd known all his life made him just as bad as his father, demanding that Alex's mother fit in with his grand aspirations.

'Let's forget about all this, eh? Go to the bathroom and fix your make-up and we'll start again, shall we?'

She nodded, blowing her nose and then frowning at the handkerchief.

'Don't worry about that. They come in packs of two. I have another one.'

He propelled her out into the hallway, where she grabbed her bag and made for the bathroom.

She was back in less time than he'd thought,

her make-up reapplied and flawless. Alex was standing in front of the mirror, trying to retie his bow tie after he'd pulled at it to loosen his collar a little.

'Let me do that. I think I have the knack now.'

She got the bow tie right first time, and folded the new handkerchief, putting it into his top pocket. A second chance to do things right. Alex picked up the velvet box, ready to put it back in the safe in his bedroom.

'Alex, would you mind…? Would you be able to perhaps lend me just the chain to wear? It's so pretty.'

She was meeting him halfway. Alex decided this wasn't the time to tell her that the workmanship on the chain was of such quality that it was considered a work of art just by itself.

'I'd like that very much. I think it's the better choice with that dress.'

He could go halfway too. Maybe that would be enough to breach the gaping chasm that seemed to have opened up between them.

He unclipped the fabulous stone from its place on the necklace, and then carefully fastened the chain around Marie's neck. 'There. What do you think?'

She walked over to the mirror. In Alex's experience, women didn't usually look this grave when trying on jewellery.

'I really like it. I'd love to wear it…just for to-night…'

Marie turned to him, smiling. And suddenly all Alex had wanted in having her wear the diamond was turning out better than expected. In choosing just to wear the chain Marie had made a powerful statement. She could take or leave one of the best-known stones in the world, but she still wanted to wear something of his.

'Tonight's going to be a little weird for both of us. We'll stick together, eh?'

She nodded. Alex stepped forward, catching her hand in his and pressing it to his lips. Not actually a kiss, it was the kind of thing his father had taught him that a gentleman would do. A royal kiss for the hand of a beautiful woman. But the sudden warmth in her eyes made the hollow gesture into something that lived and breathed.

'You look gorgeous.'

Finally Alex got to deliver the compliment he should have given when he'd first laid eyes on her. And, better still, she accepted it.

'Thank you. Shall we go?'

Marie was *very* nervous. But Alex seemed determined to get her through this one way or another. The diamond had been too much of a gesture, and the panic she'd felt when she saw it had only driven home the sinking feeling that she could never fit into his world. The kind of woman who should be on Alex's arm would have accepted the loan and given him the pleasure of seeing her wear it.

But they'd worked it out. The chain was delicate and very pretty, with silver-and-gold tendrils that made it seem as if it were almost floating around her neck. And when Alex relaxed into the back seat of the taxi and started to talk about the everyday matters that took their attention in the clinic she felt a little calmer.

The taxi took them right to the door, stopping outside the wide portico that stretched out to touch the gravel drive. The mansion was in one of the many secluded streets in central London, just moments away from the noise and bustle but surprisingly quiet. This was the territory of the rich, living cheek by jowl with everyone else, but separated by privilege and heavy closed doors.

This door was open, though. Perfume from the flowering shrubs that bordered the portico lay heavy in the air. And when she took Alex's arm, walking into the spacious lobby, the scent of wealth was all around her: beautifully waxed wooden panelling, and the smell of the fuel for the flares burning at the doorway, in the heat of the early evening.

He solved the question of when exactly she should take her coat off by stopping and helping her out of it himself, handing it to a porter. Then he made an almost imperceptible gesture and a waiter materialised with two glasses of champagne.

'Ah. There's Sonya…'

He shepherded Marie across the crowded ballroom, smiling and nodding as he went, without allowing himself to be diverted from his intended trajectory.

When Sonya saw them she waved wildly.

As always, Sonya looked as if she'd just stepped out of the fashion pages of a magazine. She wore a bright red look-at-me dress that Marie would have loved to have had the confidence to wear, with just one heavy diamond bracelet. She flung her arms around Alex's neck, air-kissing his cheeks, and then it was Marie's turn.

'You look *wonderful*!' Sonya loudly confided this information to Marie. 'I see you've managed to shoehorn Alex into looking respectable too.'

He didn't look at all respectable to Marie. She'd heard the adage that women had the same reaction to a man in a really good suit as men did to a woman in fine lingerie, and she hadn't given it much credit before now. But that exact reaction had been fizzling away inside her for a while now. Alex looked meltingly gorgeous, and the feelings that he engendered in her were anything *but* respectable.

'I'm always respectable,' Alex protested, and Sonya laughed.

'Yes, I know you are, darling, but sometimes running around saving people's lives leaves you dishevelled. You know that as well as I do.'

She turned to Marie, rolling her eyes, and Marie grinned, feeling some of the tension slip away.

Sonya took her arm. 'I suppose we'd better get to work, then. I have some very interesting people I'd like you both to meet…'

Sonya had oiled the wheels and she was making things easy. But Marie couldn't have got through it without Alex. His glances that were just for her. The way he steered the conversation, always asking first about the other person's interests without indulging his own. And when anyone asked why he was there, he spoke about the clinic, effortlessly including Marie in the conversation.

Chandeliers glinted above their heads as Marie talked about the issues that ordinary people faced, and how the clinic was being set up to address them. Under the stern eye of the lords and ladies looking down from the oil paintings on the wall, she spoke of inclusivity and the modern art that adorned the wall of the reception area, feeling the words flow naturally from her lips. And when someone who knew Alex's family asked about his plans, now that he had inherited his father's title, he said that he was taking his family traditions into new and exciting areas and left it at that.

'Did you see Sir Richard's face?' Sonya whispered in her ear as they returned together from the ladies' restroom. 'He was so impressed with everything you said, and I'd be very surprised if he doesn't want to know more. He's very influential, you know... Oh, no! You just have to leave them alone for one minute!'

Sonya came to a sudden halt, staring across the room. When Marie followed the line of her gaze she saw Alex approaching a dark-haired man in an impeccable dinner suit.

'What's the matter?'

'I didn't know Mark was going to be here. Where's Andrew?' Sonya stood on her toes, looking around for her husband.

'I can't see him. What's going on?'

Sonya puffed out an exasperated breath. 'Mark was at school with Andrew and Alex. You know that Alex was bullied?'

Marie nodded. 'Are you saying that man was the bully?'

'Yes—him and some of the other boys. Andrew told me some of the things they used to do to him and it made my toes curl. Oh, dear... I hope Alex doesn't hit him or something...'

Alex was the taller and broader of the two. One blow from him would fell the other man.

'No. It's okay, Sonya. He's not going to hit him.'

It was almost as if he'd heard her. The two men exchanged a few words, and then Alex held his hand out to Mark.

'Oh, thank goodness.' Sonya whispered the words as the two men shook hands.

Marie felt her head begin to swim. Alex must have known that this man might be here, and he'd never said a word. He was making his way back across the ballroom now, and as soon as he got within touching distance she took his arm, holding on tight.

She looked for Sonya, but she'd melted away into the crowd. She could let this go but... No. Actually, she couldn't let this go. She needed to tell Alex how proud she was of him.

'Sonya told me that man was one of those who bullied you at school.' She stretched up onto her toes, murmuring into his ear.

Alex nodded, guiding her towards the back of the ballroom, where large doors opened out onto a terrace edged by stone balustrades. As they walked down the shallow steps to one side, into a secluded garden, she clung tight to his arm.

'You did just shake his hand, right? That wasn't some kind of death grip and he's going to fall over any minute now and need urgent resuscitation?'

Alex chuckled. 'No, it wasn't a death grip. I shook his hand.'

'It was a generous act. Sonya was afraid you were going to hit him.'

'And you?'

'For a moment, maybe, but then I realised you're a lot braver than that.'

The lights of the city were beginning to brighten in the growing dusk. Here, in the quiet darkness, it felt as if they were all for her. Marie could be a queen tonight but, like Cinderella, it was only for one night. Tomorrow she'd have to give up the glass slippers and get back to work.

He let out a sigh. 'It didn't feel... When I saw him, and decided what I was going to do, I thought it might be one of those cathartic moments that changes everything. But it was a bit of an anticlimax. He seems like just an ordinary guy now.'

'Perhaps that's the whole point.'

Marie reached up, brushing her fingertips against his cheek. He wrapped his fingers around hers, pressing her hand to his chest. Everything else seemed to take a step back, the chatter of the city and the noise of the party diplomatically turning their backs on them to give them one moment alone.

'I'm so proud of you, Alex.'

The extra height her heels gave her meant that Marie didn't have to stand on her toes to kiss his cheek.

'I'm proud of you, too. I know it wasn't easy for you to come here.'

Marie shivered as she felt his lips brush her cheek in return.

Slowly he propelled her away from the path and into the dark shade of an enormous spreading tree. Marie could feel the rise and fall of his chest against hers, and as her eyes adjusted to the darkness she saw tenderness in his face.

Marie couldn't help herself. She heard his sharp intake of breath as she moved against him, brushing her lips against his. He put his arms around her, steadying her on the uneven ground, and then he kissed her.

Careful and tentative turned to demanding as a ferocious wave of pent-up desire washed over her. And Alex was already there, holding her tightly against his body as if somehow they could melt into each other and become one being.

His kiss was one that wanted it all. Everything that Marie wanted to give him.

This couldn't last. Maybe that was why it was so exciting. They both knew that these moments were stolen, and that real life would take them back soon enough.

He held her tenderly, his breath caressing her ear as he murmured words she couldn't help wanting to hear. That she was beautiful. How much he adored kissing her on a moonlit summer's night.

'So a tent in Siberia doesn't push any of your buttons?' She smiled up at him.

'You can organise the tent and I'll get the plane tickets. We'll find out.'

He obviously found the thought as interesting as she did, but she knew they could talk this way because they both knew they'd never do it. They had something that was much too important to both of them to contemplate anything more than a forbidden fantasy.

'Or we could go to Egypt. Ride out into the desert on camels… Or to Paris and climb the Eiffel Tower…'

'We could. And there's always Camden. Hoxton. Maida Vale…'

The familiar names sounded suddenly exotic on his lips. Alex would make anywhere exciting, and his kiss would be equally intoxicating.

'Or we could go back inside. Finish off the job we came to do.'

'That would be good, too. In a completely different way.'

Alex's arms loosened around her waist. They both knew this had to end, and that they'd never go to Siberia or Egypt or Paris together. That Camden, Hoxton and Maida Vale would seem perfectly ordinary in the morning.

He was the one who had the strength to move, to take the first step back. Marie had his arm, but when they emerged from the shadows she stopped.

'Lipstick.' She pointed to her own mouth, to indicate where the smear was on his, and then pulled the handkerchief from his pocket, shaking out the folds and giving him the end that would be hidden when it was refolded.

'Did I get it all?'

'Bit more.' Marie took the handkerchief and wiped tiny smudge from the side of his mouth.

'Thanks. You've got some…er…' He waved his finger in a circle, pointing at his own face.

That wasn't a lot of help. Marie was sure she didn't have lipstick in her eyebrows. She wiped her lips, deciding she would go straight to the ladies' room and repair the rest of the damage.

'Okay?'

He nodded, offering his arm again. Marie took it and they walked together back up the steps to the terrace. They had a job to do, and it didn't involve kissing.

CHAPTER TEN

LAST NIGHT HAD been a mixture of emotions: wanting to protect Marie and the horrible suspicion that one of the things he needed to protect her against was him; meeting Mark and finding that he was an ordinary man and not an ogre; the feeling that if Sonya made any more introductions he was going to go out onto the terrace and yell for mercy.

And also sheer, unthinking delight.

Alex had tried to convince himself that their kiss was something that happened between friends. Out of curiosity. Like the way that, as boys, he and Andrew had kissed the backs of their own hands, to practise what it might be like to kiss a girl.

But kissing Marie had been nothing like kissing the back of his hand.

He felt a little less awkward at seeing Marie again than he might have done. She'd made it easy—going back to the party with him, slipping her hand into the crook of his arm just as she had before. They'd talked about the evening in the taxi together without mentioning the kissing part. And then they'd said their goodnights and he'd watched her to her door.

It was over. Done. And even if it couldn't be forgotten they'd both put it behind them because it was impossible to do anything different.

He saw Marie strolling across the front courtyard now, chatting to Zack. She seemed happy, smiling in the late-morning sunshine.

Alex quickly got the papers he was supposed to be working on out of his briefcase and laid them on his desk to make it look as if he had actually been doing something. He heard a knock on his door and then Zack entered, leaving a respectful distance between himself and the desk.

'Is it okay if I help Marie, please? She's going to do some more wall-painting.'

'Yes, of course, Zack. Thank you very much.'

Alex wondered whether Marie would decide to do all her communicating with him via her brother today. It was a possibility.

But as Zack turned to go Marie popped into the doorway. 'Charlie and a couple of the other guys are here. They've come to help for a few hours.'

'That's nice of them. Tell Charlie I'll be along soon.'

'I'm sure he could do with a hand from his number one apprentice.' Marie grinned.

'Yep. As soon as I've checked the accounts I'll be there.'

Alex could almost manage to look at her without thinking about last night. The softness of her lips...

'Here...'

She had something in her hand, and she tossed it towards him. Alex caught it, opening his fist to see what it was.

'That's exactly what I need. Thank you.' She'd brought him an eraser in the shape of a dinosaur.

Then she was gone. Alex congratulated himself on not embarrassing either her or himself, and turned his attention to the papers in front of him.

Half an hour later, he scribbled his signature on the last page, and was about to write a note to the accounts manager, when Zack came bursting into his office.

'Come and help... Marie...'

Panic and breathlessness had rendered Zack capable of alarming Alex, but not able to tell him where he needed to be.

'Zack!' Alex stood up taking him by the shoulders. 'What's happened? Where's Marie?'

'Over the road—at the site office. Charlie went over there for something and didn't come back. Marie and I went to find him...'

That was enough for the time being.

Jim knew the letting agent for the small row of shops across the road, and he'd negotiated the use of an empty one as office space and storage while the works at the clinic were being carried out.

'We called him but he didn't answer...we looked through the front window and his hat was there...we banged on the door... Marie broke in...'

Zack was breathlessly recounting the story, running behind him as Alex crossed the road. He didn't need to know any of that. Just that Marie and Charlie were all right.

The door of the shop was open, and there was a bent piece of wire that Marie must have shoved through the letterbox to flip the lock. Alex cursed under his breath. Why hadn't she come to fetch him?

Because she could do it herself.

The warm, pliable woman who had clung to his arm last night, to balance herself over the uneven ground in her high heels, was more than capable of doing what needed to be done this morning. That was what he loved about Marie...

There was no time to consider his use of the word *love*. Alex noticed Charlie's bright red baseball cap, propped on one of the drawing boards by the window, and hurried past the desks and storage boxes to the open door at the back, which led to the stairs. He could hear sounds of effort, followed by a loud crack, and then a clatter.

He ran headlong down the stairs. At the bottom he saw Marie's face, shining up at him.

'Alex. Thank goodness!'

He resisted the impulse to hug her. 'Are you all right? Where's Charlie?'

'Inside. I heard him.' She gestured towards the door that led into the basement. 'But I can't get the door open—there's a pile of stuff behind it.'

She'd made a good start. The door stood open a few inches, and the light was on inside. Alex could see a mess of plaster from a broken sack and pieces of wood piled against the other side of the door, which stopped it from opening any further. Marie had found a crowbar from somewhere, and had managed to lever the bottom hinge away from the doorframe.

She wasn't tall enough to get good leverage on the top hinge, and nor was she strong enough to move the heavy door, which was now hanging on just one hinge. Alex took the crowbar, inserting it as far as it would go between the door and the jamb.

'Hold that in place.'

Marie stretched up to grip the crowbar, and Alex felt Zack jostling at his back.

'Zack, get out of the way, will you?'

Zack jumped back, giving them some room.

Alex jerked the door closed, bracing his foot against the door, and holding on to the handle.

'A bit further...'

When he pushed the door open again he could see that the hinge had given a little. Marie slid the crowbar further into the gap and he pulled again. This time it gave, and he grabbed the other side of the door before it fell forward.

'Zack, mind out.'

Marie stepped back, taking Zack with her as Alex tipped the door forward, turning it slightly so that it would fit through the frame and then backing with it into the lobby.

Before he could stop her Marie had slipped past him and into the basement, climbing over the sacks of concrete mix that had slipped from a pile further inside the room and blocked the door. Dust hung heavy in the air, and there was a mess of spilt paint cans, brushes and other supplies, which had come from the heavy timber shelves that had once lined the wall. The shelves must have collapsed, because there was splintered wood everywhere.

'Charlie!'

She picked her way across the debris to where Alex could see Charlie's red T-shirt and fell to her knees.

'He's hurt, Alex. We're going to need an ambulance.'

Zack was ready to pile into the room and help, but Alex pulled him back. 'Go upstairs, Zack. Call an ambulance and tell them there's been an accident and to hurry. When you've done that, I want you to fetch the medical kit from the urgent care room in the clinic and bring it down to us.'

'But… Marie…' Zack's eyes were full of frantic tears for his sister.

'Do you want me to stand here arguing with you, or shall I go and help her?'

Zack nodded, pulling himself together suddenly. 'Look after them, Alex.' He threw the order over his shoulder as he ran up the stairs.

He would. Both Marie and Charlie.

Marie was vaguely aware that Alex was making his way across the piles of debris towards her. She'd heard Charlie crying out when she'd first reached the door that led into the basement, but now he was still and unresponsive, the lower half of his body pinned down under a pile of rubble.

'Airway?' Alex was there beside her.

'He's breathing and his airways are clear. I don't see any major bleeding…' She leaned forward, finding Charlie's wrist. 'And his pulse is surprisingly steady.'

'Okay, stay with him, and I'll move some of this wood away from his legs.'

Marie nodded. She'd known that she couldn't

get the door open by herself and had hoped that Zack would find Alex quickly. Together they would be able to help Charlie, and now they'd fallen automatically back into the habit of depending on each other to get the job done.

'Glad you're here.'

'Yeah. Glad *you're* here.'

Alex set to work, clearing the mess of paint cans and smaller pieces of wood from around Charlie's legs. Charlie was alive. All they had to do now was keep him that way.

Marie bent over him, smoothing his hair from his brow and tapping his cheek with her finger. 'Charlie! Charlie, can you hear me?'

Charlie moaned, moving his arms as if to push whatever was holding him down away. Marie caught his hand, holding it tightly in hers.

'Charlie. It's Marie. Look at me.'

As Charlie opened his eyes he let out a long, keening cry of distress.

'Charlie, I want you to stay still, if you can. Just look at me.' Marie clung to his hand, trying to calm him.

'I can see his legs,' said Alex. 'The right one looks okay…'

Which meant that the left one didn't. But Alex would tell her if he needed her, and Marie concentrated on Charlie's pulse, beating beneath her fingers.

'It hurts…'

'I know. We'll have you out of here soon, Charlie. You're doing really well—just hold my hand.'

'Yeah. Hold on.' Charlie groaned as Alex carefully lifted the piece of wood that was lying across his leg.

One more piece to go, and then Alex would be able to see better. It was a big piece, though—one of the shelves that had fallen from the wall. Marie glanced up at Alex and he nodded.

'Charlie, Alex is going to move the last piece of wood. It's going to hurt, so hang on to me.' She bent over Charlie, so he wouldn't see what Alex was doing.

Alex positioned himself in order to take the strain, and carefully lifted the heavy shelf. Charlie howled in pain, his fingers digging into Marie's arms.

'Okay. Okay, we're done. That's the worst bit over, Charlie.'

She could see his left leg now, twisted and certainly broken. Blood was pluming out over his jeans and dripping onto the concrete beneath him.

Alex leaned forward, gripping the top of Charlie's leg, putting pressure on the main artery to stanch the flow. His other hand found Charlie's, gripping it just as tight.

'Where's the medical kit?' Alex muttered the

words, looking up as movement in the doorway indicated that Zack was back.

Marie broke free from Charlie and picked her way across to Zack. He was standing staring at Charlie's leg, and looked as if he was about to faint.

Marie grabbed the medical bag from his hand. 'Is the ambulance on its way? Zack!'

'Yes… I told them to hurry.'

'Good. Well done. Now, go back upstairs and wait for them outside. Got it?'

'Yes. Yes, I can do that.'

Zack straightened suddenly, and Marie turned him around, pushing him towards the door. Her little brother had been thrown in at the deep end, but he was doing fine.

She opened the medical kit, sorting through the contents of the bag to find a pair of surgical gloves and scissors. Alex was talking to Charlie, trying to reassure him while he did what he could to slow the bleeding. Carefully cutting Charlie's jeans, Marie exposed the wound on his lower leg.

The broken bone was sticking through his flesh, blood pumping out around it. There was no way that Alex could put any pressure on the wound to stop the bleeding.

'Tourniquet?'

Alex nodded. Marie took the tourniquet from

the bag, looking at her watch and writing the time on the tab.

'Let go of Alex, Charlie. Hold *my* hand.'

As soon as Alex was free to work he wrapped the tourniquet around Charlie's leg. The bleeding slowed and then stopped, and Alex turned his attention to check that there was no other bleeding.

By the time the ambulance crew arrived they were ready to move their patient. Alex helped them to carry Charlie through to the small goods lift at the back of the building, and he was transferred into the ambulance.

'I'll go with him.' Alex moved towards the back of the ambulance.

Marie caught his arm. 'You're sure?' She knew the ambulance paramedics could be trusted to look after Charlie.

'He's my responsibility.' Alex's jaw was set firm.

It was a bit of a stretch to feel that any of this was Alex's responsibility, but there was no talking him out of it. He and Charlie had struck up an unlikely friendship, and Alex wouldn't let him go to the hospital alone.

'Okay. I'll call Jim and get him to contact Charlie's family. When you're done, give me a call; you can't walk back looking like that.' She nodded towards the blood on Alex's jeans.

He looked down, seeming to see it for the first

time. 'Yeah, okay. Thanks. Zack did well. Don't forget to tell him that.'

'I won't.'

Zack had been frightened, but he'd done everything he'd been asked. Marie wondered whether her little brother would have been able to do that before he'd come to work here, and was proud of how far he'd come.

She watched as Alex spoke to the paramedic and then got into the back of the vehicle. The doors closed and the driver climbed into her seat. There was a short pause, and then the ambulance drew away from the kerb.

Jim had arrived at the hospital with Charlie's parents. About ten minutes later Charlie's older brother and his wife had come bursting through the doors of the waiting room.

Alex had sat them all down and explained what had happened, and the surgeon's prognosis. Charlie would need an operation to set his leg, and he'd be in hospital for a few days, but he had no other major injuries. The bruise on his face looked distressing, but it would heal.

When Charlie's mother saw her son her hand flew to her mouth, but she steadied herself and walked over to his bed, kissing him. Charlie's father shook his hand and thanked him, and Alex knew that it was time for him to leave.

He called Marie and then sat on a bench outside the A&E department, adrenaline and concern for Charlie still thrumming in his veins. All he wanted to do was hug Marie—but he saw Zack walking towards him from the direction of the car park.

'I said I'd come. Marie needed to wrap things up at the clinic.' Zack settled himself down on the bench next to him, asking the obvious question. 'How's Charlie?'

'They'll need to set the leg, and that means—'

'An operation and he'll be here for a few days. Yeah, Marie told me. They didn't find anything else?'

'No. He's got lots of cuts and bruises, but he'll be fine.'

Alex grinned. Marie had obviously talked everything through with Zack and he seemed to be taking it all in his stride.

'When can we go and see him?' Zack peered at the doors of the A&E unit, obviously wondering if he might go in and see Charlie now.

'His family are with him, and we shouldn't interrupt. I'll call tomorrow, and you can take some time off in the afternoon if he's up to having visitors.'

'Great. Thanks. I'll make the time up.'

'That's okay. I think it counts as official clinic business. Charlie's one of ours.'

Zack nodded, his face suddenly thoughtful.

'What, Zack?' Alex leaned back on the bench, ready to listen to whatever Zack had to say.

'It's nothing really. I just…' Zack turned the corners of his mouth down. 'I didn't know what to do.'

'Your sister's a doctor. She's been trained to know what to do.'

Zack nodded. 'Yeah, I know. But… I was afraid. I said we should phone someone to come and let us in. If we'd done that Charlie might have bled to death. She was so brave the whole time, and nothing stopped her. I didn't know she knew about breaking and entering.'

'The coat hanger trick?' Alex grinned again. Marie hadn't actually used a coat hanger, but she'd found a piece of wire that had done just as well. 'I taught her that years ago.'

'Really?' Zack gave him a searching look. 'It was *you* that led her astray, then?'

Not really. Getting Marie into her student flat—when he could have asked her back to his place for the night—could be construed as *not* leading either of them astray. But Zack didn't need to know that.

'You did well, Zack. You did what we needed you to do and let us work.' Alex held out his hand, reckoning that Zack needed something a little more definite than words. 'I'm proud of you.'

'Thanks.' Zack brightened suddenly, shaking Alex's hand. 'You know, Marie's always looked after me... Mum too. A bit too much sometimes.'

That was Alex's opinion, too. But he had no business saying it.

'I'm going to take more responsibility for things. I'll pay her back every penny of the money I took. I want to make a difference, the way she does.'

Alex laid his hand on Zack's shoulder. 'You made me proud today, Zack, and I'm sure your sister feels the same way. And, yes, you *are* going to keep working until you pay her back.'

Zack nodded, getting to his feet. 'She'll be wondering where we are. I'll drive.'

Marie's jeans were still spattered with blood, but she'd washed the grime from her face and hair, and cheered up considerably when Alex gave her the exact details of Charlie's condition.

'He was lucky. How on earth do you think it happened? Everything coming down on top of him like that?'

'Jim told me that he caught him climbing up those shelves the other day, to get something at the top. He gave him a dressing down—told him it was dangerous and said he should use the step-ladder. But I guess Charlie didn't listen.'

Marie quirked her lips. She knew as well as

Alex did that there was no saving people from themselves. 'What about the mess? Should we go and clear up a bit?'

'That's okay. Jim's been on the phone to a couple of his guys and they'll take care of it. I think we're done for today.'

Neither Marie nor Zack argued. Alex claimed the car keys from Zack, saying that they'd drop him home, and Marie directed him to a neat two-up, two-down terraced house with a riot of colourful plants in the front garden.

'I'll come in with you...' Marie went to get out of the car but Zack reached forward from the back seat, grabbing her.

'I'll deal with Mum.'

Marie frowned. 'Are you sure? You can't just tell her about it and then disappear up into your bedroom. You know she worries.'

'I'll make her a cup of tea and talk to her. You're not the only one who knows how to do that, you know.'

'No, I know.' Marie grinned suddenly. 'Okay, then, Zack. See you tomorrow?'

'Yep. Bright and early.'

Zack shot Alex a grin and then got out of the car, loping up the front path and turning to give them his characteristically ebullient wave.

Alex put the car into Drive and accelerated away before Marie could change her mind.

'He did well today.'

Marie didn't ask where they were going, and Alex decided to head for his flat. Maybe he could make her lunch.

'Yes. He told me he wanted to make the kind of difference that you make.'

'That's nice.' She smiled. 'Mum tells me that he's got a severe case of hero-worship. "Dr King says this…" "Dr King did that…"'

She was twisting her fingers in her lap, clearly thinking about something. Alex wondered if it was the kiss, and hoped not. In between dealing with Charlie, he'd been thinking about it enough for both of them.

'I was wrong.'

'Were you?' In his view Marie was perfect. 'What about?'

'I thought that if I worked hard enough then I could fix things. I could pay Mum back myself and persuade Zack to buck his ideas up. But I couldn't. I had to stand back.'

'That's the most difficult thing sometimes. Not that I'd know—I don't have a great deal of experience with families…'

Marie was so involved with her family. That might have its difficulties, but she felt a part of them. Indissolubly linked. Alex had worked for most of his life to distance himself from his family.

'You know people, though.' She reached forward, pulling her phone out of her handbag. 'Mum hasn't called me yet. I suppose that's a good sign...'

'Put it away, Marie. Give Zack a chance to deal with things. I know you've always been there for him, ever since he was little, but maybe it's time to let go now.' Alex ventured it as a suggestion.

'What? And have a life of my own?'

She made it sound like a joke, but Alex knew she'd got his point, and that she was thinking about it.

He shrugged. 'Funnier things have happened.'

'Yes, they have.' She gave a little sigh. 'I couldn't do what you did, Alex—taking Zack on like that and giving him direction. Thank you.'

A warm feeling spread through Alex's veins, making his hand shake a little on the wheel. He felt as if he'd been part of something good, and in his experience good things didn't happen in families.

Suddenly the idea of driving Marie home and leaving her there seemed impossible.

'It's Sunday afternoon. Would you like to go for a late lunch somewhere?'

'Like we used to?' Marie smiled.

'Yes.'

Driving out into the country would be good.

He'd lost something from those days and he wanted it back.

'I can't go anywhere like this.' She pointed to the grime and blood on her jeans.

'We could drop in to your place.' Or, better still, he could avoid Marie's flat entirely so she didn't get a chance to change her mind. 'Or I could lend you a pair...?'

Apparently they called the style 'boyfriend jeans'—rolled up at the bottom and cinched tight at the waist. But Alex decided that he didn't need to be her boyfriend to lend Marie a pair of jeans, and that plenty of women wore the manufactured version.

'You've got diamond-encrusted jeans?'

Marie giggled suddenly, and Alex realised she was teasing him. 'Yeah. It was all the rage in eighteenth-century Belkraine.'

'This I have to see...'

CHAPTER ELEVEN

THE NEEDLESSNESS OF Charlie's accident, the repeated wish that he'd applied a bit of common sense, or a least listened to what Jim had told him, was beginning to be set aside now, along with her worry about Zack and her mother. This afternoon there was just Alex—and he was irresistible.

There had been a bit of awkwardness about who should go where to get changed, which Alex had solved by laying out a pair of jeans for her in his bedroom and then going to get changed and take a shower in the bathroom.

She could hear the sound of water running, and tried not to think about the inevitable consequence of that. Alex...soaking wet and naked.

Resisting Alex had always been hard, but she'd grown used to it. Now that she'd felt his touch it was a whole new ball game. And now that some of the responsibility for Zack and her mum had been lifted from her shoulders there might be time to indulge her fantasies.

But it was too risky. They were friends and colleagues and they were both at turning points in their lives. Anything could happen and they would smash all that they'd built together.

She rolled up the legs of the jeans, cinching the waist tight. They didn't look so bad with her flat canvas shoes, which had thankfully escaped any specks of blood. Her lace-edged sleeveless shirt was fine on its own, and now that the sun had burned away the early-morning cloud she didn't need the zipped hoodie she'd been wearing.

She walked back into the sitting room. Perhaps Alex had always looked her up and down like that but she'd never noticed, and it made her heart jump. His smile was even better.

'Diamonds really suit you.'

She laughed, and the joke loosened the tension between them. Alex picked up his car keys, hooking his sunglasses onto the front of his shirt, and Marie put her purse in her pocket. They were ready to go, travelling light the way they'd used to do. Just the open road and what they could carry in their pockets.

He left the clinic's car to charge in the basement garage under the flats and they took his car. With the top rolled back, raw power purring from the engine and a warm breeze caressing her skin, this felt a lot like sex. Although she reckoned that sex with Alex would be a lot better.

After a drive that was enough to blow the most stubborn of cobwebs away they found a picturesque pub in a picturesque village and ordered lunch to eat in the garden. The artisan burgers weren't quite as nice as they'd looked on the menu, but it didn't matter. They were taking the world as it came.

'Careful…' said Alex.

Marie had slipped off her shoes, putting her feet up on one of the plastic chairs, and luxuriating in the sun. 'Careful of what?' She opened one of her eyes, shading her face so she could see him.

'You'll catch the sun. Might even look as if you've been on holiday…' He smirked at her.

The last holiday she'd been on had been the summer before her father had left. Since then, the only thing that had seemed remotely like getting away from it all had been the times when Alex had persuaded her away from her books and out into the sunshine.

'We can't have that, can we?' She wrinkled her nose at him.

He chuckled. 'Too late. I think I see a touch of pink on your shoulder.'

'Oh, no!' Marie pretended to brush it off and Alex laughed.

'Do you want to tell me about your plans for the open day? It's only two weeks away.'

'Not right now.' Marie stifled a yawn. 'This

is our afternoon off. We can go through them tomorrow.'

'I never thought I'd hear you say that. *Mañana* has never been your thing.'

Marie let the idea roll for a moment. *Mañana* never *had* been her thing, but that was because there'd always seemed to be so much to do.

'I might take it up. Take a break once every month or so.'

'Yeah... I wouldn't overdo it—you might find it becomes a habit. *Then* where would you be?'

If all her breaks were like this one she would be...happy. Marie dismissed the thought. However alluring it was, it was a fantasy.

They spent another hour in the sun together, and then Alex suggested that a film might fill the evening nicely. But after they'd driven back to his place and consulted the listings they found there was nothing that either of them particularly wanted to see.

'Shall we download something to watch?'

'That would mean making a decision, wouldn't it?' Marie was too relaxed to move.

'Yep. Good point.' He grinned, reaching for the remote for the sound system and switching it on. 'Random will do...'

'Random' did very nicely. Some soul, some rock and roll—a bit of everything.

Marie's foot started to tap against the leg of the

coffee table and suddenly Alex was on his feet, catching her hand.

'You want to dance?'

She hesitated, and he shot her an imploring look. He picked up the remote and suddenly the sound swelled and the beat became irresistible.

Alex was irresistible.

Marie stood up and he swung her round, away from the sofas and towards the clear space to one side.

Alex was a great dancer. He had always moved well, and he danced without any of the tense awkwardness that made sitting it out the best choice with some partners. They seemed to fit together, anticipating each other's next steps, and by the time the rock and roll track was finished she was out of breath, falling laughingly into his arms.

There was a moment of silence in which she looked up at him, felt his body against hers, her chest rising and falling with excitement. And then the next track started.

'I love this one…'

'Me too.'

He wrapped his arms around her and they started to sway slowly to the music. Each movement was perfect. There was nothing more that she needed.

Then she felt his lips brush the side of her forehead, and realised there *was* something more she needed. She tipped her face up towards his, stretching her arms around his neck.

This was better than last night. They were truly alone, without having to worry about lipstick or someone strolling into the garden and discovering them. She could feel his body, hard against hers, still swaying to the music. But now there was another, more insistent rhythm, which gradually began to take over.

'Alex…'

He moved from her mouth to her neck, and she felt herself shudder with pleasure. Pulling at the buttons of his shirt, she slid her hand across his chest, feeling muscle move under soft skin.

They were breathing together now. He gasped as she tucked one finger under the buckle of his belt, knowing that this was a statement of intent. She intended to make him feel everything that she did.

Suddenly he lifted her off her feet. Marie wrapped her legs around his waist, feeling the hot surge of desire suddenly let loose after far too long spent denying it. He took a step and she felt her back against the wall, his hand curling protectively around her head.

'Alex…' She fumbled for the heavy belt around her jeans, trying to pull it off. 'Now. Please…*now*.'

It had to be now. While she was still lost in the powerful force of trembling expectation.

Suddenly he stilled. And as he let her gently down onto her feet he planted a tender kiss on her brow.

It was gone. The moment was gone.

'We can't, Marie. Not like this.'

One of his arms was braced against the wall above her shoulder. He seemed to be pushing himself back, away from her.

What did he mean? Not like *how*? Marie stared up at him, frustrated longing bringing tears to her eyes. She was too scared to say anything.

He picked up her hand, pressing it to his lips. 'I want to make love to you, Marie. But if we rush at it before we have a chance to think and change our minds… I need to know that you're not going to regret this when you do get a chance to think about it.'

He'd known her haste was borne of uncertainty. That they had a lot to lose. A friendship that had lasted for years. Their work together.

He turned away from her suddenly and flipped the remote. Silence. Picking up the keys of the clinic's electric car from the coffee table and then putting them into her hand, he closed her fingers around them.

Alex wouldn't tell her to go. He didn't want her to go—she could see that in his eyes. But if she stayed, it had to be a real decision. They couldn't just let themselves be carried away by insistent desire.

They could go back now. Pick up on Monday morning and keep working together. Working together was their strength and anything else was a weakness. They could stick with what they were good at or…

They could want more.

Suddenly, she knew. Marie put the car keys down onto the coffee table. 'Alex, you're my friend, right?'

'Always. You know that, Marie…'

'We both have regrets about the past. You wish your mother had left, and I wish my father had stayed. And although we're so different we've always talked about things. I feel that whatever happens we can work it out.'

He didn't move. 'Is that a yes?'

'I trust you, Alex. It's a yes.'

The heat of his gaze was more exciting than the heavy beat of the music had been. More arousing even than his touch.

'I trust you too. My answer's yes.'

Marie stepped forward, undoing the buttons of his shirt that she hadn't already torn open. He didn't move, letting her slip it from his shoulders. When she ran her fingers across his chest he caught his breath, stifling a groan.

He reached for her, pulling her vest over her

head in one swift movement that made her gasp. He traced the edge of her bra with his finger, bending to kiss her neck, and Marie felt her knees start to shake.

'Alex…?'

Just moments ago this had been unthinking desire, but now it was a true connection. If he severed it now she didn't know how she would survive.

'I've got you.'

He understood everything. He understood all her fears. And she understood his, and they'd face them together.

Alex picked her up in his arms, carrying her along the hallway and kicking the bedroom door open.

They undressed each other. Alex had thought about this so many times before, but never dared go there. He wasn't in the habit of sleeping with girlfriends on a first date, but he'd never known someone so well. The challenge was so much greater, and yet the rewards might be equally so.

It would be all right. He'd dreamed his dreams, and now that Marie held them in her hands he knew that they were safe there.

'I never imagined you'd be so exquisite.'

He'd lingered over taking off her underwear and they were both trembling now. She flushed with pleasure. Her fingertips were exploring his body, her gaze fixed on his. This was the first time he'd made love to a woman who really knew him.

'You're the only one, Marie, who knows who I am.'

'I'm not going to call you Rudolf.' She whispered the words. 'I prefer Alex.'

'So do I.'

He lifted her up, feeling the friction of their bodies healing him. He knew exactly what to do now. When he tipped her back onto the bed she gave a little cry of joy that made him feel like a king. A *real* one.

She was reaching back, her hand feeling behind her to the curved wooden headboard. Alex grinned, warming to the task of making it as hard as possible for her to concentrate on anything but him, and she moaned, her body arching beneath his.

Long minutes of teasing ensued, but finally she managed to do what she'd set her mind on. Marie knew that about him too. She hadn't forgotten that late-night conversation between five young doctors during which Alex had declared that the best place to keep condoms was taped to the back of the headboard. Always handy to reach, and never in the way.

She pressed the packet into his hand. He

wouldn't normally reach for them so soon, but he knew they were both ready now. They'd waited for this for years, and there was no denying it any more.

'I can't wait any longer, Alex. We've waited too long already...'

CHAPTER TWELVE

ALEX WAS THE kind of guy who liked to talk. Marie liked that, because he knew what to say and he also knew exactly when to stop talking.

The first time, he'd been as careful and tender as any new lover should be. It might have lasted hours if it hadn't been for the groundswell of emotion making every gesture into something that had taken them both to the very edge. When he'd pushed gently inside her they'd both known there was no going back. And when the moment had come it had gripped them both with the same splintering, tearing pleasure, ripping the world as they'd known it apart. Marie could pretend all she wanted, but things were never, ever going to be the same again.

He'd held her in much the same way as he was holding her now—curling his body around her as if she were finally truly his. They should have drifted off to sleep, but it had still been early, and light had been streaming in through the windows. Marie had felt more awake than she'd ever felt, and Alex had murmured comfortable words until shared jokes and whispered tenderness had become spiked again with longing.

That seemed like a very long time ago now. They'd made love and slept in equal measure for hours, and now it felt as if his body and hers belonged together.

'You're awake?' Marie shifted slightly in his arms as he spoke.

'I'm too comfortable to open my eyes. What's the time?'

She heard him chuckle and felt the brush of his lips against her cheek. 'Four o'clock. We don't have to get up yet.'

'Hmm… Good.' They'd been in bed for ten hours already, but Marie didn't want to move. Not yet.

'I really liked ten o'clock…'

Marie opened one eye. 'You were looking at the time?'

'You're not going to tell me that you didn't hear the clock chiming in the other room, are you?'

'Yes, I heard it. Was that ten?'

'I counted ten. Did you lose count?'

The innocence in his tone made her smile. As the clock had chimed ten she'd been astride him, and he'd taken hold of her hips, moving suddenly in the same rhythm as the sound. Marie had got to three and then lost count. A couple more thrusts and she'd started to come so hard that ten hadn't even existed.

Alex knew how to break her, and he knew how to be broken. Marie had always felt that was what sex must be all about, but this was the first time she'd allowed it to happen with anyone. He knew how to make her beg, but he had no hesitation in putting himself at the mercy of her touch.

'So what's four o'clock going to be?'

She snuggled against him, dropping a kiss onto his lips. They really shouldn't be doing this. They should both be considering the benefits of an IV drip to combat exhaustion by now.

'I can't imagine.'

The glint in Alex's eye told her that he probably could imagine and that he was doing so right now.

Marie closed her eyes again. 'Surprise me.'

His arms tightened around her and he pulled her back against his chest. Already desire was beginning to make her tremble.

'You like this…?'

One of his hands had covered her breast and the other was moving downward, nudging her legs apart. He held her tight, dropping kisses onto her neck.

'Yes, Alex!'

She wriggled, trying to make his fingers move a little faster, and heard his low chuckle.

'Four o'clock is all for you…'

* * *

At six in the morning there was the smell of coffee. Alex had left two cups on the table beside the bed, and was gently kissing her awake. They wished each other a drowsy good morning, and Marie reached for a cup.

'Mmm. That's better.' Neither of them spoke again until the caffeine began to kick in. Then she said, 'I should be going soon.'

Alex turned the corners of his mouth down. His expression of regret was just what Marie wanted to see.

'I've got to go home for a change of clothes and a shower.'

She didn't want to go either, but the idea of turning up to work in Alex's jeans was impossible. The dress code at the clinic was relaxed, but that was a little too relaxed, and someone was sure to notice.

'You won't shower with me?'

Tempting. 'We could try to leave *one* thing for next time.'

Voicing that fantasy had prompted a slip of the tongue and turned into a suggestion that there *would* be a next time. Neither of them had broached the subject; last night had been an exercise in the here and now, and no forward planning had seemed necessary.

He grinned suddenly. 'I'm hoping that means

you're not going to break my heart and tell me that this is the first and last time this is going to happen.'

Break his heart? Marie left the thought where it belonged, along with all the other professions of love spoken in the heat of the moment.

'I want a next time, Alex.'

'Me too.' He gathered the scattered pillows and leaned back against them, putting his arm around her. 'It's not going to be easy to keep everyone from noticing at work today.'

'We could just stay in our offices.'

Marie didn't really care if everyone knew, but it was common sense not to advertise the fact when you were sleeping with someone you worked with—especially not until you knew exactly where the relationship was going.

'Nah. That's not going to work. When two people suddenly start avoiding each other at work, the first thing everyone thinks is that they're sleeping together.'

'Hmm. True. How about being so busy that we don't have time to think too much about it?'

'Might work.'

He thought for the moment. 'Although I'm not sure I can sustain that level of busy for more than a couple of hours. I guess we'll just have to wing it.'

He took the cup from her hand, putting it down on the table.

'Alex! Not again!'

'We have time. You could be half an hour late for work, couldn't you?'

'No, I couldn't. And neither could you. What kind of example is that?'

He chuckled. 'It's a dreadful example. We shouldn't do it...' His eyes flashed with boyish mischief as he raised her hand to his lips.

'There you go, then.'

She really wanted to stay...just for another fifteen minutes. But temptation was there to be resisted.

Marie pushed him away, and he flopped back onto the pillows, laughing.

'Can I at least watch you dress? Crumbs to a starving man...?' She was picking her clothes up from the floor.

'You are *not* starving, Alex.'

He couldn't possibly be—not after last night. She pulled on her underwear, and then his jeans, belting them tight around her waist. Then she crawled onto the bed, keeping the crumpled duvet between his body and hers.

'One kiss.'

'Just a kiss?' He grinned at her.

'Yes. No cheating, Alex...'

He held his hands up in a gesture of surren-

der. Those hands were his most potent weapon.
She dipped down, planting one kiss on his lips,
thrilling at his sigh of disappointment as she left
him, hurrying into the sitting room to find her
top and shoes.

She drove home in the clinic's electric car, with
the radio playing and Alex's scent still on her
body. Even after she'd showered it felt like she
was still his. He'd claimed her, and she couldn't
escape by merely being apart from him.

She dressed, drying her hair in front of the
mirror. There was something different...some-
thing she couldn't quite put her finger on. Her
expression made her look like the cat that had
got the cream, and try as she might she couldn't
persuade her face to assume her usual smile.

But Marie need not have worried. When she
saw Alex at the clinic, he smiled his usual greet-
ing. He made the Monday morning meeting easy,
not seeking out her gaze but not afraid to meet
it. He acted as if last night had never happened.
If anyone should divine that something earth-
shaking had happened to her over the weekend,
they never would have connected Alex with it.

It was slightly unnerving. Marie didn't want
anyone to know any more than he did, but her
vanity felt he might have made this appear a little more difficult.

But it was just the way Alex was. He was

protecting his privacy and hers. He'd grown up learning to maintain a face for the world that didn't show any of his true feelings, and it had become a matter of habit for him. She shouldn't confuse that with the real Alex. The one who'd made love to her last night, who'd listened to her heart calling him, and whose heart had replied so eloquently.

Alex had phoned the hospital and the news was good. Charlie's leg had been operated on yesterday afternoon and he was recovering well. Zack was eager to visit him, and Alex had said he'd go too. Marie had decided that three around his bed might be a little too much for Charlie, so she contented herself with packing a bag full of things he might need, along with a few treats, and had given it to Zack to take in.

'So how is he?' When Alex walked into her office later, she breathed a sigh of relief that she no longer had to pretend to work while she waited for them to get back.

'He's okay.' Alex closed the door behind him and sat down. 'He's pretty sore and he's got a real shiner. But I spoke to his surgeon and he'll mend.'

'Great. That's good.'

Marie wondered if she was supposed to keep the pretence up now that they were alone. Perhaps the rule was that they only referred to last night when they were off clinic premises.

'I saw his mother as well. I told her we'll provide whatever Charlie needs in the way of rehab and that either you or I will personally oversee his case.'

'Good. Thanks. She's happy with that?'

Knowing what to do with her hands was a problem. She'd known exactly what to do with them last night, but that wasn't appropriate here.

'She asked me to thank you for everything you did yesterday. Charlie might well have bled to death if it hadn't been for your decisive action.'

Marie's heart was beating even faster than it had been. Rolling a pencil round and round in her fingers took the edge off the tension a little. 'It's…you know…'

He grinned. 'Yes, I know. All in a day's work.'

So far there was nothing. Not even any of the in-jokes that they cracked all the time. Marie could do this. She just wished that there was one hint from Alex that he hadn't already left last night behind. That he didn't regret it.

'I've sent Zack out to get an MP3 player and a decent pair of headphones. Charlie's phone got smashed in the accident and the hospital radio doesn't play his kind of thing.'

Marie frowned. 'What is his kind of thing?'

'I'm not completely sure. Zack's going to help

me with that; we'll download some music for him after work. You want to join us?'

Something sparked in his eyes. Maybe it was just the mention of music, and the prospect of exploring a few new artists. But even if it was just that, the thought of spending a few hours with two of her favourite people was incredibly tempting.

'I can't—sorry. I'd like to, but I promised I'd call round and see Mum after work. She wants a chat.'

A crease formed on Alex's brow. 'Okay.'

It wasn't okay with Marie. She wished now that she'd asked her mother whether it really needed to be tonight, instead of just automatically acquiescing. But that was what she'd always done before.

'We'll miss you.'

What would have happened if he'd said that before? All the times when their friends at medical school had gone to play softball in the park, or gone to the pub to talk out a long day's work.

Marie dismissed the idea. She'd always tried not to think about the things she was missing out on, and concentrate on the things she needed to do instead.

Suddenly he got to his feet, leaning across the desk towards her. Meeting Alex's gaze was hard, because his grey eyes held all of the promise of last night. It wasn't over between them.

'Could I persuade you to come back to mine after you've seen your mother?'

The pencil snapped suddenly in her fingers. Marie jumped, dropping it onto the desk, and saw the edge of Alex's mouth curve.

'Yes. That was what I had in mind, too.'

'You want to snap pencils with me?'

'All night.'

'I might be late... I won't get away from Mum's before about nine.'

'I'll wait. I have a spare door key downstairs; you can let yourself in. And take one of the clinic cars—you'll get back to me sooner...'

'It's an emergency?'

'Yes.'

He brushed a kiss on her lips and her whole body went into overdrive. Definitely an emergency...

It was ten o'clock before Alex heard the key turning in the door of his flat. He'd decided to go to bed and allow himself to doze a little before Marie arrived. She'd know where he was.

She did. He heard her footsteps in the hallway and the light outside being flipped off. The warm glow of the lamp in the corner of the bedroom threw shadows across the floor.

Alex watched as she took her clothes off. No words. She knew he couldn't take his eyes off her, and it seemed that her movements were slower and more deliberate than usual. She took the time to hang her dress carefully across the back of the easy chair that stood next to the lamp, and he devoured the shadows that played across her body.

When she was naked, she walked over to the bed. She hesitated, as if she'd forgotten something, and then ran her fingers across one breast and down towards her stomach. The sudden urgent wish to take her now crashed over him, but he resisted it. Waiting would make the having so much better.

'Get into bed…'

His words sounded suspiciously like an order, which made Marie smile. Her movements seemed to slow even more and Alex grinned. She knew exactly how to tease him.

When she slipped under the duvet he moved towards her, wrapping his arms around her but keeping thick layers of down between them. He could tease too.

Alex leaned forward, planting a kiss on her mouth, and she let out a gasp.

'Everything okay?' He smiled innocently at her.

'Yes. Mum just wanted to say how pleased she was about Zack.' She turned the corners of her mouth down. 'She could have said that when she called me.'

Alex resisted the temptation to agree. He loved the way that Marie was so close to her family, and wished he could have had a measure of that himself. It was hypocritical to say that he wished they'd give her a bit more time to herself. Because what he really meant was that *he* wanted her time.

'We've got a few hours to catch up on...' she said, disentangling her arm from the duvet, caressing the side of his face.

'Hey... You know I don't mind if you've got something else to do.' Tearing Marie in two wasn't going to solve the problem—it would only make things worse.

'I know you don't. But *I* mind.'

The thought shattered the last of his self-control—that Marie had wanted to give up the responsibilities that she clung to so ferociously in favour of this.

He pulled the duvet away from them and rolled her over onto her back, covering her body with his. She could see and feel how much he wanted her.

'Where do you most want to be now?'

He wanted to hear it. If she screamed it out, then all the better. He wanted every moment she spent with him to be time that she didn't want to be anywhere else.

Her eyes darkened suddenly, the light playing that trick he loved so much and turning them to midnight blue. Marie reached behind her, giving an impatient huff when she remembered that they'd used all the condoms taped to his headboard last night. Her fingers searched the surface of the bedside table until she found the packet he'd bought on his way home.

He gritted his teeth, waiting while she fumbled with the wrappings. Then she reached down, and he felt his blood begin to boil as she carefully rolled the condom into place.

When she took him inside her it felt as if he was coming home after a long journey. He stared into her eyes, watching every small movement, listening to the way her breathing started to quicken and match his as he pushed deeper.

One moment of stillness.

They spent it wisely, feeling the warm sensations of being together at last.

Then Marie's lips parted. 'Here, Alex. I want to be right here.'

CHAPTER THIRTEEN

ALEX HAD ENVISAGED a rather sedate affair for the clinic's open day—a Saturday afternoon spent coaxing people in with the promise of free coffee and then showing them around to give them an idea of what the clinic could offer to the community.

Marie had dismissed that idea with a wave of her hand and started to search the internet for someone who could supply bunting.

Alex knew that Marie thrived on organising this kind of thing and he'd passed the preparations to her, taking over her clinic caseload for a week while she appeared and disappeared, off on various missions to secure the things that they simply couldn't do without. When they were alone at night he got her undivided attention. Alex had always reckoned that sex was a pleasant addition to a relationship, but when he had Marie in his arms it was more important than breathing.

He arrived at eight in the morning the day of the open day, six hours before the doors were due to open, and found that a bouncy castle was already being set up on the grassy area at the back of the clinic. When he walked into the café, he found Marie supervising a couple of Jim Armitage's men, who were manoeuvring a piano into place.

'Where did you get this?' Alex ran his finger over the wooden frame. It was a good one, and had clearly been polished recently.

'I found it in the outhouse where Jim puts all the things you ask him to get rid of.' She tapped her nose, in the way that Jim did when he was about to impart a pearl of wisdom. 'You never know what might come in handy.'

'I thought it was just old pieces of wood. What else is in there?'

'Loads of stuff. I found one of those old-style blackboards, with a wooden stand. You should go and take a look sometime. This was from the school music room.' She opened the lid that covered the keyboard. 'I had it tuned.'

Alex hadn't seen or heard the coming or the going of a piano tuner. Marie's innocent look indicated that she'd probably kept that activity well away from his notice.

'What are you going to do with it?'

Alex supposed it might make a nice piece of furniture for the café. Marie had added a few things in there to make the clean lines into a more welcoming area.

'Well, we could always play it. We've got some people coming to sing this afternoon; I thought it might help break down a few barriers.'

'So that's where you and Zack disappeared off to the other evening. Auditions?'

Marie nodded. 'I've got an a capella group. A few of them are backing singers for other bands, and they look and sound marvellous.'

'Great.' Alex had no doubt he'd approve of her choice.

'Why don't you try it out?'

She opened the lid that covered the piano keys and Alex reluctantly jabbed a couple of notes with his finger.

'Sounds as if it has a good tone.'

Marie rolled her eyes. 'Come on, Alex, I know you can play.'

Long hours at the piano when he was a child had seen to that. But Alex didn't play any more. Apart from just that one time…

'I don't think Christmas carols are going to be appropriate for today.'

She rolled her eyes. 'I don't know all that much about music, but I know that anyone who can play Christmas carols with the kind of tempo that gets a whole ward full of kids singing along can play pretty much anything.'

That had been a good evening. A Father Christmas had turned up from a local charity, but no one had admitted to being able to play the piano that had stood in the corner of the family room on the children's ward. Alex had sat down, and the kids' faces had made him forget for a while that all the piano meant to him was rapped knuckles.

'I haven't played for years.'

She flashed him an imploring smile. 'It's like riding a bike, isn't it? Do you know this one?'

She started to sing, her voice wavering up and down, somehow managing to hit every note but the right one. He grinned. Marie had never been able to carry a tune, and it was yet another thing that was perfect about her. But he could recognise which song she meant from the words and he picked it out with one finger.

'That's the one.' She gave him a thumbs-up.

He'd do anything to make Marie happy—even this. So Alex sat down, trying a few chords and then moving down a key. That was better. He was rusty, but he could still play.

Alex operated the volume pedal and added a little oomph to the tune, gratified at the way she smiled, moving to the music. He improvised, adding a few extra choruses. He was enjoying watching her.

When he'd finished, a muffled round of applause came from the kitchen.

Marie shot him an I-told-you-so look. 'That's great. I wish you'd play more.'

Alex was almost tempted. But in a world where everything seemed to be changing he had to hang on to a few of the rules he'd made for himself when he'd left home.

'I don't have good memories of playing the piano. You wouldn't either if you'd been at one of my father's music evenings. Twenty adults, all staring at you, just waiting for you to make a slip.'

'It sounds awful, Alex. But you love music—you always have. You have a talent, and you can't let anything take that away from you. And…well, the a capella band did tell me they have a couple of numbers that they usually sing with backing tracks…'

'Even if I wanted to, I can't just sit down and play for them. There's such a thing as rehearsal.'

Marie shrugged awkwardly. 'They'll be here soon to set up their equipment. There's plenty of time before we open the gates to the public.'

Alex sighed. 'Have I just been set up?'

She capitulated so suddenly that he almost hugged her. Marie was the one person he couldn't resist, and her transparency made her all the more seductive.

'No. Well…yes. But not really. The band have a recorded backing track they can use.'

'So that's not quite a yes. But it's not a no, either.'

She gave him an agonised look. 'I always

wondered why you didn't play—you're so good. When you told me about your father I put two and two together. But this is…it's *your* place. You should fill it with your sound. Of course, if you really don't want to…'

He held up his hand and Marie fell silent. 'Send them through when they arrive. I'll help them set up their equipment.'

'So that's a yes?'

'Not quite. But it's not a no, either.'

'Okay. Good.'

She gave him a ravishing smile and hurried away.

Marie could have made more of a mess of that, but she wasn't sure how. Although Alex hadn't seemed too cross, and he was at least going to talk to the a capella band.

There was plenty left to do. She had to make sure all the examination rooms were locked, and call Sonya to check that she had their special guests in hand. Then rescue Zack before he got himself completely buried under piles of bunting, and make sure the cafeteria staff had everything they needed…

The bouncy castle was inflating nicely, and when the band arrived she sent them through to the cafeteria. Zack appeared, red-faced and grinning, declaring that the bunting was finally all under control.

'Who's playing the piano?'

Soft strains of music were floating through into the reception area. A few chords, and then a woman's voice, singing a few bars and then stopping as player and singer began to adjust to each other.

'Um... Alex, probably.'

'He plays?' Zack took a few steps in the direction of the music. 'I've got to see this.'

'No, I need you here.' Marie frowned at her brother.

'But...'

'Help me get these display boards up.'

This was something Alex needed to do on his own for a while. The woman's voice had begun to swell, more powerful now, and she could hear Alex beginning to follow her lead. They didn't need any interruptions.

Zack pulled a face. 'Okay, where do you want them...'

The countdown seemed to fly by. Sonya arrived, along with the special guests she'd promised to bring—a footballer and a runner—who ceremonially opened the gates at two o'clock to let the small crowd that had gathered in.

The sun shone, and more people came. The sound of voices and music echoed through from the cafeteria, and the two celebrities set up shop in the reception area to sign autographs and smile for an endless number of photographs.

The clinic staff were all busy showing small groups around and answering questions, the café was packed, and the bouncy castle was a big hit with the children. People were sitting out on the grass at the back of the clinic, just enjoying the sun. Sonya had the reception area well under control, and Alex was nowhere to be seen.

When she heard the singers stop for a break, and the strains of the piano drifted through from the cafeteria, Marie smiled. Finally she felt that she might join him.

The lead singer of the a capella group, a shy woman who suddenly became a force of nature when she opened her mouth to sing, was standing by the piano, tapping her foot and drinking a glass of lemonade. When she put her glass down and nodded to Alex, he smiled, working the music around to what seemed to be an agreed point, when the woman started to sing.

It was breathtaking. Full of energy and soul. And both of them were clearly enjoying themselves.

Marie sat down in the corner of the cafeteria and Zack hurried up, putting a cappuccino down on the table in front of her before turning to help the serving staff. Everything was under control.

This was what the clinic was all about. A community helping each other. It was about Alex too. She'd asked him if he thought that the clinic would save him. Watching him here, it seemed that it just might.

Saturday had been great. Sunday had been delicious and lazy. Monday was nerve-racking.

'Are you nervous?' she asked.

Alex didn't look a bit nervous; he looked handsome and dapper in his dark blue suit.

'Terrified. You?' He shot her a smile across the bedroom.

'I don't think this dress is right. And my jacket's far too bright...' Her make-up was probably wrong as well, for a TV appearance, and Marie hoped that part of the reason they had to be at the studio hours before their scheduled appearance was because they would fix that.

'You look gorgeous. Anyway, the whole purpose of a dark suit is to show off the woman next to you.'

Marie wasn't sure that made her feel any better. She'd rather fade into the background and have Alex take the glare of the attention they were hoping to generate.

'I'm a doctor, Alex. Not a mannequin.'

'Who says you can't be a stunningly beautiful doctor? The two aren't mutually exclusive.'

'Stop.' She held her hand up. 'I know you mean well, but you're not making this any easier.'

'Does this?'

He walked around the bed, enveloping her in the kind of careful hug that was designed not to crease their jackets, but still felt warm and reassuring.

'What happened to being able to do anything together?'

'It's live TV, Alex!'

'We've built a clinic and we can do this.'

Marie nodded, disentangling herself from his arms and smoothing the front of his jacket. He was steady and secure, like a rock. She just had to remember not to hang on to him too much in public, however much she might want to. She knew Alex wasn't ready to let that mask of his slip yet. He guarded his private life fiercely.

The car arrived to take them to the TV studio and they drove through clear streets, bathed in early-morning light. She slipped her hand into his, knowing that this was breaking all their rules about keeping their relationship strictly behind closed doors, but not really caring. Alex's touch might be subtle, and he didn't kiss her fingers the way he had before they'd left his flat, but it was enough to keep her from panicking and trying to jump out of the car when it stopped at a red light.

A cheery make-up girl applied lipstick in a

shade that seemed too bold for Marie, explaining that it would look much the same as her normal colour under the lights of the studio. They were shuffled from one place to another by various production assistants, and finally they walked onto the set.

Alex was standing to one side, to let her go first, but still keeping protectively close. The presenters of the morning show beamed at them, murmuring a few words of encouragement. They were clearly used to dealing with nervous guests.

First there was a short film about the clinic that had been made earlier in the week. Sonya had picked out all the elements which were most important in the accompanying press release, and the questions were easy enough. Alex answered his with exactly the kind of friendly approachability that they wanted to be the hallmark of the clinic, and Marie managed to get through hers without stumbling.

It was going well. She kept her gaze on the two presenters, trying not to look at Alex. She knew he was there with her, and that gave her courage.

Then the female presenter leaned forward, smiling at Alex. 'I believe that it's your inheritance that has made the clinic possible, Alex?'

Too close for comfort. But Alex's face didn't show any of the dismay that Marie felt.

'I count myself fortunate in having been able to use it to do so.'

'And as you've also inherited a royal title...' the presenter paused for effect '...I think we can all agree that you're one of London's most eligible bachelors now. Is there any chance that we have a royal wedding to look forward to?'

The woman was being deliberately challenging. Marie wondered whether strangling her on live TV would be considered an appropriate response, and glanced up at Alex.

His smile didn't change. 'I'd far rather everyone saw me as a doctor. One who's working a little too hard to contemplate romance at the moment.'

'You're sure...?'

The male presenter shot a pointed look at Marie, and she wondered whether her body language had given her away. She'd been so frightened that maybe she'd unconsciously sat a little too close to Alex on the sofa.

'I'd love to think that there's a woman out there who could put up with me.' Alex's tone took on an appropriately rueful note. 'But I'm still waiting to find her.'

The female presenter laughed, looking quickly at the overhead screen. 'Well, I think we have a few offers coming in already on our social media feeds. Thank you, Alex and Marie, for being with us this morning.'

A new topic was started, and the programme cut to a filmed report. The two presenters thanked them again, and they were hurried off the set. Marie's heart was beating so fast she could hardly breathe.

As soon as they left the glare of the cameras Alex's face turned ashen. Marie grabbed his arm. 'Not a word…' she said. Not until they could talk privately.

He nodded down at her. The kind of decision-making that had seen them through so many medical emergencies would get them through this one.

They walked back to the small dressing room where they'd left their things, and quietly managed to elude anyone who might stop them. The receptionist called after them, asking if they were going to wait for their taxi there, and Marie gave a smiling shake of her head while Alex kept walking. As soon as they were on the pavement he hailed a taxi, and to Marie's relief the driver saw him and stopped to pick them up.

'I suppose it was going to happen sooner or later. I'll speak to Sonya,' Alex said. His whole body was tense, as if he was waiting for some new blow to appear from somewhere. 'It can't hurt the clinic so much now. We've started to establish ourselves in the community and people know what we're about. We just have to hold on to our values and try to keep the press away.'

Clinic first. Always. But this had to hurt Alex. He'd spent so much time leaving his past behind, and now it had come back to haunt him in the most public way possible.

'My father would have *loved* this.' There was a trace of bitterness in his voice. 'Just think—all he had to do was one good deed and the press would have come snapping at his heels.'

'He missed a trick there.' Marie tried to lighten the mood between them, and Alex smiled grimly.

They both knew that with a little careful management this wouldn't compromise their work at the clinic, but it had raised a question that neither of them wanted to answer just yet. If Alex was going to be caught in the media's spotlight, what would happen to their relationship?

Alex fell silent, his face clouded with worry. When the cab drew up outside his mansion block he paid the cabbie and wished him a good day. He didn't say another word until they were inside his front door.

'I'll protect you. I'll make sure none of this touches you,' he said.

Marie suppressed the urge to shake him. 'What if I don't want you to protect me?'

'This isn't the time, Marie. I know you can do

everything by yourself, but things would be a lot easier if you'd let me help.'

Her face was itching from the heavy make-up and suddenly all Marie wanted was to be alone. 'I'm going to wash my face...'

He nodded, and she escaped to the bathroom, washing her face and splashing it with cold water.

Sonya had been right. Alex's royal heritage and his determination to do something good with it was a great story. He was one of the most eligible bachelors in London, and of course there would be interest in his love life. What had she been thinking when she'd got involved with him?

She'd been thinking about his touch. About how they got each other, as best friends *and* as lovers. She hadn't been thinking about the practicalities, about how when the news became public she'd be standing with him in the glare. About how she'd cope with navigating his world when she had no compass.

She wanted to get out of these clothes. She went to the bedroom, changed into a pair of comfortable trousers and a shirt. She heard the phone ring and the low resonance of his voice.

'No. No comment... You can speak to Sonya Graham-Hall about any publicity matters to do with the clinic. You have her number... No, I really don't have anything else to say...'

When she went back into the sitting room the

jack for the landline lay unplugged on the floor and he was holding his mobile against his ear.

One minute...

He mouthed the words, holding up his finger to indicate that the call wouldn't last long, and then spoke into the phone.

'Hi, Sonya. Did you see it?'

Suddenly Marie didn't want to listen to this. She went into the kitchen and set the kettle to boil, making two mugs of tea. When she heard Alex stop talking, she walked back into the sitting room.

'Thanks.' Alex was in full damage-control mode now. He took the tea, putting it down on the coffee table in front of him. 'I've spoken to Sonya, and she's going to field all the press enquiries for now. We don't answer any questions from anyone.'

'Okay.' That sounded sensible enough. 'So what do you think we should do?'

He pressed his lips together. 'I don't see that we have much choice. We don't see each other for a while—until this all blows over.'

'I have a choice. I can stand by you.'

'You don't want this, Marie. You've told me yourself that you're not comfortable with my royal status, and it's about to get a whole lot worse.'

'I never said that!' Marie reddened. She'd demonstrated it, though, by refusing to wear the diamond. Actions spoke louder than words.

'Are you going to tell me you'd be happy with that kind of notoriety?'

'No. But I don't have to be happy with it, Alex. If it's who you are then that's what I'll be.'

'That's…'

His gaze softened for a moment, and Marie though he was about to relent. Then steel showed in his eyes again.

'I've seen the damage that can do, and I won't let you do it, Marie.'

'But I *want* to do it. I don't want to be the kind of person who thinks the best thing to do when things get tough is to walk away. My father did that, and I've been dealing with the consequences ever since.'

That was the difference between them. It wasn't just a matter of lifestyle—although it terrified Marie to think she might be catapulted into a world where she felt like a fish out of water. They'd both lived through different versions of an unhappy childhood, and they'd always have different solutions for life's problems.

Tears suddenly blurred her vision, burning like acid. Maybe the answer to this was that there *was* no answer. That there was nothing either of them could do to make it right.

He got to his feet. 'Perhaps we should talk

about this later. I have to go over to see Sonya, to work up a press release. Just the basic facts; she reckons that'll give us some breathing space.'

That was probably wise. It would give them both a little time to cool off. Although in truth Alex looked perfectly cool now. He'd switched off, retreating behind the mask he'd worn all his life—the one he'd hidden behind as a child, which had protected him from his past ever since.

'Yes, okay. You'll go back to the clinic?'

'Yes, I'll see you there.'

He turned away. When Marie heard the front door close it sounded just the same as it always did. She'd almost prefer that he'd slammed it—at least it would have given some hint of what was going on in his head.

She should go to work. By the time Alex returned to the clinic she'd be calm. And when they came back here they'd go to the bedroom and forget all about their differences.

Maybe.

Marie picked up the overnight bag into which she'd folded her dress and jacket, collecting up the other odds and ends that had found their way here and putting them into it too. A comb and a tub of moisturiser. A book that she was only halfway through, which lay on the kitchen table. The pages were creased at one corner from where it had been dropped on the floor, discarded when

Alex had leaned over to kiss her and passion had made her forget everything else. Tears pricked at the corners of her eyes and she stuffed it quickly into her bag.

She didn't need to do this. Gathering up her things seemed so final…as if a decision had been made. People argued all the time…

But Marie couldn't see the way back from this. As she closed his front door behind her the click of the latch seemed to mark an ending.

Alex's meeting with Sonya lasted half an hour. She'd seen that he couldn't concentrate, and had kept it short and simple. 'Just tell me what you want and I'll handle it,' had just about covered it.

He took a taxi back to his flat, but Marie was already gone. That at least gave him some time alone, to think. He just wanted to take shelter from a world that wanted to know nothing about *him* and everything about his royal connections.

Running to the comfort of Marie's arms would ease his pain, but it was the same as hiding inside the walls of the clinic. If he was going to protect them—Marie and the clinic—he had to distance himself from them both for a little while.

Sonya would manage things, and a few well-chosen media releases and interviews would draw the press away from the gates of the clinic, so their patients didn't have to run the gauntlet of photographers. It would draw them away from Marie, as well, so she didn't have to face the bright glare of publicity.

Marie would never forgive him if he walked away. She'd told him already that she would stand by him, but he'd never forgive himself if her commitment to the job, to the clinic, to his dream, meant she had to change in an attempt to fit in with what she thought was expected of her.

If he stayed he'd lose her completely, but if he left there was a chance that their friendship might survive.

For the last few weeks he'd been beyond happy, and he'd allowed himself to think that maybe he did know how to make a relationship different from his parents' marriage. But he'd fallen at the first hurdle.

When he finally made a move, changing out of his crumpled suit and making his way back to the clinic, he knew what he had to do. Marie was in a staff meeting that was due to last for the rest of the afternoon, and he waited until Tina, the receptionist, popped her head around his office door.

'Everyone's gone for the evening. It's just you and Marie.'

'Thanks, Tina. Have a good evening.'

'You too. Are you okay…?'

Tina shot him a puzzled look, and Alex nodded

and smiled back at her. The last thing he wanted was to make his relationship troubles the talk of the clinic.

He heard the front doors open and then slam shut again. He had to do it now. Before his courage failed him and wanting Marie took over, driving everything else from his mind.

Alex walked upstairs, feeling his burden increase with every step. Marie's office door was open and he stopped in the doorway, afraid that if he went in and sat down he wouldn't be able to do this.

She looked up from the papers in front of her and her eyes seemed suddenly hollow, as if she hadn't slept for a week. 'You're back.'

'Yes.'

No invitation to come in and sit down. It seemed Marie had nothing to say to him—which was fair enough because he had nothing to say to her. They'd always understood each other, and they understood this as well.

He took a breath. 'I think we should stop. For good. We'll tear each other to pieces if we don't.'

She nodded. 'Yes. I think so too.'

That was the most difficult part and it had been achieved in a matter of a few words. Alex bit back the temptation to fall on his knees and beg her to fight him. That would just prolong the agony, because he and Marie had never been meant to be together.

'I'm going to bring forward my trip,' he said.

The trip had been planned for him to scout out sites for new clinics around the country. It was an ideal excuse to get him away from London for a couple of weeks.

'After that I'll be concentrating on development, so I'll be working from home most of the time.'

'But… No… I'll clear out my things. There are plenty of jobs for qualified doctors in London. I'll just call an agency and I'll have another job by the weekend.'

She was regarding him steadily, her lip trembling and her eyes filling with tears. This wasn't what he'd meant to happen at all.

'What? No, Marie. We always kept our private lives separate from our work before. You can't leave.'

He knew he was in no position to tell her what she could or couldn't do. Thankfully Marie overlooked that.

'I'm not sure I can stay, either.'

Alex thought fast. It was beyond unfair that a broken relationship meant Marie felt she had to walk away from her job. If she decided to leave he'd make sure she was paid until the end of the year, but that wasn't the point. She'd put her heart into this place and given it life. It was as much hers as it was his, and she'd see that once the initial shock of their parting had subsided.

'Stay for a couple of weeks at least. I need you to be here while I'm away. We can talk again when I get back.'

She nodded. 'All right. Just until then, Alex.'

It was almost a relief to walk away from her, so he could no longer see the pain in her beautiful eyes. He'd never wanted to hurt Marie, but all he'd brought her was sorrow. He'd come to love this place, but he'd give it up a thousand times over if it meant she would stay.

He needed her in his life, and he hoped desperately that in time they'd learn to be friends again, but he was beginning to doubt that. There was no coming back from this.

CHAPTER FOURTEEN

IT HAD BEEN ten days since she'd seen Alex. He'd walked out of the clinic that evening and Marie had been able to hold back her tears only just long enough to hear the main doors close downstairs. Then she'd got unsteadily out of her chair and walked over to the corner of her office. Sliding down the wall, she'd curled up on the floor, sobbing.

But they'd done the right thing. They needed completely different things from a relationship, and it never could have worked. That didn't mean it hurt any less.

The emails had started the following day. Alex's first one had been short and polite, and Marie had replied in the same vein. They'd loosened up a little as the days went by and his itinerary took him further and further away from London. Maybe after a year or so one of them might crack a joke.

She missed him so much. Her head wanted him and her body ached for him. Sofia Costa had asked if she was coming down with something, and Zack had noticed too.

'What's up, sis?' He wandered into her office now, carrying a packet of sandwiches, and plumped himself down, offering her one.

Marie took it, wondering whether he'd made extra this morning just for the purpose of sharing.

'What's this?' She peeled one of the slices of bread up. 'Ah...cream cheese and cucumber. Thanks.'

Zack nodded. He knew that was one of her favourites. 'I've made egg and bacon as well.'

Zack was definitely on a mission to spoil her. Marie smiled at him, grateful for both the sandwiches and his concern. Her little brother had come a long way in the last few months.

'Is something going on? Between you and Alex?' he asked.

'What...?' Marie almost choked on her sandwich. 'What makes you think that?'

'Well, he's never around any more. You know that's always a sign there's something going on... when two people start avoiding each other at work.' Zack nodded sagely.

'Where did you get that from?' Clearly not from his own experience; Zack hadn't managed to hold a job down for more than a week before he came here. Marie wondered if people at the clinic were talking.

'It was in a film on TV. Two people started an affair and all the people at work knew because they suddenly started being really horrible to each other.'

'Well, I'm not having an affair with Alex.' That was strictly true—she wasn't having one with him any more. And she wouldn't be having one with him in the future, either. 'And he's not been around because he's in Edinburgh at the moment, talking to people about possible sites for a new clinic.'

'Only half an hour away by air... You were looking pretty tired on Monday—'

'Stop!' Marie brought her hand down onto her desk and Zack jumped. 'I haven't been sleeping so well recently.'

Zack frowned. 'So what is it, then?'

'Nothing. Really.' Marie decided this was as good a time as any to tell Zack. 'I'm going to be leaving the clinic.'

Zack's eyes widened in shock. 'But why? You love it here.'

'It's...not what I thought it would be. I'm not with the patients as much as when I was working at the hospital.'

'I thought you liked it? You know...developing stuff. Finding solutions.'

She did. But it was the only reason that Marie had been able to think of which didn't involve talking about her split with Alex. She wasn't able to do that just yet without dissolving into tears.

'It's a lot of paperwork. But, Zack, this won't affect your job here. That's between you and Alex, and my going won't make any difference.' Marie knew Alex would honour his agreement with Zack, whatever happened.

Zack thought for a moment. 'I want to stay. I like it here.'

And Zack had been more than pulling his weight. He'd turned into an asset for the clinic, and people were beginning to depend on him.

'Like I said, my leaving doesn't make any difference to your position here.'

'Okay. Thanks.' Zack was obviously a little unhappy with this, but he'd run out of questions to ask. Instead he offered her another sandwich. 'Bacon and egg?'

'Thanks. I'll keep it for later, if you don't mind.'

Their email conversation hadn't been an easy one, but Marie had been determined. She couldn't stay at the clinic. Even when Alex wasn't there everything about it reminded her of him. She had to make a clean break. And it wasn't fair that he was staying away, because she knew he loved the place. He'd built it and she wanted him to have it.

He'd protested, but she'd stood firm, because she knew it was the best thing for both of them. They'd agreed that she should stay on for another week, until he was back, and that he'd take on her current medical and management duties after that.

It was where he was supposed to be. It was where he'd always intended to be, and Marie was just making things right.

She cleared out her office, trying not to cry over the box of pink paper clips and the lava lamp that Alex had given her. Then she said her goodbyes to everyone and left. Alex would be coming to the clinic tomorrow, and she wouldn't even lay eyes on him.

The next two weeks were hard. She missed Alex every day. She missed the clinic every day. But she kept going, cleaning her flat from top to bottom and applying for jobs. Running in the park, with the express purpose of exhausting herself so that she'd sleep. Sometimes it worked and sometimes it didn't.

But today was a good day. There were two emails asking her to job interviews. The sun was shining. She still missed Alex, but even that was beginning to subside from a sharp, insistent pain to a dull ache. Her life would never be the same without him, but it could still mean something. She could still make a difference.

She replied to both the emails, saying she'd be there at the times stated, and sorted through her wardrobe to find a suitable outfit. Her red jacket might go nicely with a plain dress, but that was still in her overnight bag, creased and crumpled. Marie hadn't been able to bear opening it to go through all the things that had once been at Alex's flat.

The doorbell rang and she pressed the Entryphone. That would be Zack. She opened the front door of her flat and went into the kitchen to put the kettle on. She heard footsteps on the stairs, and then a quiet knock on the door.

'Come *in*, Zack.' Why was he messing around knocking at the door?

'It's not Zack.'

Marie froze. Alex's voice. When she looked out into the hallway she could see him, standing outside the open door.

He looked tall, tired and handsome. Marie swallowed down the lump in her throat, willing her heart to slow down, but it ignored her.

'Alex… I'm sorry, I was expecting Zack.'

Polite was the way to go. They'd been ruthlessly polite in their emails and that had worked. Perhaps it would work in person, too.

'I wanted to talk to you. I asked Zack if he knew whether you'd be at home this morning.'

Light suddenly dawned. Zack had called her, asking if she'd be in, because he had something for her. It was Alex. Seeing Alex again was what Zack had for her. She was going to kill him.

'Well, come in.' She switched on a smile that didn't feel even vaguely natural. 'I dare say I've got things mixed up.'

He was holding the soft leather briefcase that he used for his laptop and papers. Perhaps he needed to speak to her about something to do with the clinic, in which case she was going to be professional. She wouldn't cry, and she wouldn't hold on to him, begging him to stay.

'Thanks.' He stepped into her hallway, closing the door behind him. They were standing twenty feet away from each other, but suddenly he seemed very close.

'I'll make coffee. Go and sit down.'

She motioned him towards the sitting room and he nodded a thank-you. Good. Two minutes to breathe deeply and try to recover her composure.

By the time she carried the coffee into the sitting room she was feeling a little giddy. Maybe the deep breathing had been a bad idea.

'What can I do for you?' She didn't dare say his name. Not after she'd whispered it so many times to herself in the dark hours of the night. 'Something to do with the clinic?'

'No.'

He opened his briefcase, reaching inside and producing a large thick book, bound with an elastic closure. He put it down on the coffee table, laying his hand on it as if he were about to swear an oath on it. Whatever the oath was, it seemed to be a matter of some importance to him; he was looking unbearably tense.

'This is my life. Everything about me. It's for you.'

She stared at him. Perhaps he'd been in therapy and this was his homework. If that was the case, she wished it hadn't brought him here to seek closure.

'The final pages are blank…'

'Alex, I'm not sure this is a good idea.' Closure was going to take a little longer than this for her. Her whole life, if the last few weeks were anything to go by.

'They're blank because I want you to write them with me. We both want the same things, but we've both struggled with a way to find those things. I love you, and I believe we can find a way together.'

It was as if the sun had just emerged from behind a cloud. Light streamed into a very dark place.

'You love me?'

'Yes, I do. Tell me now if you don't feel—'

'I love you too, Alex.' Now wasn't the time to listen to him work his way through any of the other options. 'I always have.'

He leaned forward, stretching out his hand. Reaching for her across the chasm that divided them.

'I've always loved you too, Marie. I couldn't put the past behind me, and that broke us apart. But I want to make this work and I'll do anything to be the man you want. I'll stick by you always, whatever happens.'

Marie reached for him, putting her hand in his. 'And I'll never give in to you. You'll never make me into someone that I'm not.'

He grinned suddenly. 'I know. I shouldn't have underestimated you.'

She could feel herself trembling. All she had to do was give herself to him, and it was the only thing she wanted to do. She and Alex could do anything they wanted...

'I only want you, Alex. Just as you are.'

The urgency of her need to be close to him took him by surprise. Marie bolted across the top of the coffee table and fell into his arms, kissing him. He caught his breath and then kissed her back with the same hunger that she felt.

'Just as I am? Crown and all?' His lips curved into a delicious smile. 'You're sure about that, now?'

'I'm sure.'

When he kissed her again, it all seemed wonderfully simple.

* * *

It was the best day of Alex's life. They were both finally free.

Marie had reached for the book he'd been labouring over for the past couple of weeks, pulling it onto her lap, but they hadn't been able to stop kissing each other. It had slipped unnoticed to the floor when he lifted her up to carry her to her bedroom. She'd practically torn off his clothes, and he'd been just as eager. If this was what commitment was like, then he was its new biggest fan.

'What do you want to do? Apart from spending the rest of your life with me…?' he asked. Marie had told him that already, and he'd voiced his own pledge. He belonged to her, and he always would.

'Mmm…' She stretched in his arms. 'I want to shower with you and then look at my book.'

Her book. It was her book now. His memories, his life, were all hers.

Alex loved it that Marie found it important enough to choose a bright summer dress from her wardrobe and apply a little make-up, just to look at it. It gave it a sense of occasion.

She laid the book on the small dining table at one end of her sitting room, along with a couple of photograph albums from her own shelves. Then she sat down, opening the first page of the book.

'Oh! I think you might just be the cutest baby I've ever seen!' Marie reached forward, flipping over the cover of one of her own albums. 'That's me.'

'So you were born adorable, then…?'

It took hours to go through everything. But it felt as if they were slowly taking possession of each other. As if Marie was saving him, and he could save her.

'Are you hungry?' By the time they finished it was late in the afternoon.

She nodded. 'Why don't we go out somewhere and eat? Anywhere. Then we could go to the seaside.'

'We'll drive down to the coast and find somewhere to stay for the night.' Alex grinned. Just the two of them. No baggage, just his car keys and his credit card, and maybe a change of clothes. 'There's something I want to do first, though.'

He went to fetch the velvet-covered box from his briefcase, putting it in front of her on the table. She recognised it immediately, and raised her eyebrows quizzically.

'I didn't tell you all you should know about this.'

He opened the box and the large diamond

glinted in the sunshine that filtered through the window.

'Go on.'

'This diamond is called Amour de Coeur.'

'It has a name?'

'Most large and well-known diamonds do. It was given by one of the more enlightened Kings of Belkraine to his wife, a few hundred years ago. They were very famously in love, at a time when a king's marriage wasn't really about love. And although she had her pick of all the other royal jewels, she only ever wore this one.'

'It's a beautiful story.'

'Will you dare to wear it, Marie?'

Alex could hear his own heart beating. She caught her breath, and then she smiled.

'I'd be proud to. It's a part of your heritage so it's a part of me, now.'

She reached forward, running one finger over the large diamond and the beautiful filigree chain. Suddenly the jewels of Belkraine and Marie's smile—which outshone them all—seemed to go naturally together.

'I have one more diamond for you.'

He got up from his seat, falling to his knees before her and taking her hand in his.

She let out a gasp, knowing exactly what this was.

'Alex!' Tears began to roll down her cheeks.

'Will you marry me, Marie?'

'Yes!' She flung her arms around his neck, forgetting all about the diamonds.

The ring had been burning a hole in his pocket, but it wasn't the thing that sealed their loving covenant. It was Marie's kiss.

'Will you let me go?' He finally managed to tear his lips away from hers.

'No. Never.'

He chuckled. 'Just long enough for me to do this properly...'

Alex took the ring from his pocket. It wasn't the biggest diamond in his inheritance by a very long way, but it had been carefully chosen and was one of the best in quality, flawless and slightly blue in colour.

'I'm starting a new tradition.'

Her eyes widened. 'What? Tell me!'

'My tradition is that when the King of Belkraine wants to marry he takes one diamond from the royal diadem, replacing it with another gem.'

'That's...from a crown?' She pointed at the diamond ring. It was modern and simply fashioned, made to Alex's exact specifications.

'Will you make it yours? We'll take our inheritance and mould it into something that we're proud to pass on to our children.'

She held out her hand and Alex slipped the

ring onto her finger. Suddenly everything fell into place. Their love…his inheritance. All that they wanted to do with their lives. It was all one.

She laid her hand on the book filled with pictures of him as a child. 'I want a baby that looks just like you.'

Alex chuckled. 'And I'd like one that looks like you. We can work on that.'

She hugged him close. 'Can we run away together now? To the seaside.'

Alex kissed her. 'There's nothing I'd like better.'

Alex took Marie to the old manor house in Sussex a few weeks after their engagement. She recognised the carefully laid out gardens and the brickwork around the massive doorway from the photographs in the book he'd made for her. She held on to his hand tightly as he showed her around.

'What do you think?' His brow creased a little as he asked the question.

'It's…okay…'

She loved the Victorian knot garden, the Elizabethan rooms with their nooks and crannies and large, deep fireplaces, the massive banqueting hall which had been turned into a sitting room, big enough to hold a beautiful grand piano at one end. The decor left a lot to be desired—it was far too ostentatious for Marie's taste—but the house was a pure delight.

'You love it, don't you?' He shot her a knowing look.

'A house with a maze in the garden? I'm sure there'll be lots of interest when you put it up for sale.'

It was a wonderful, magical place. But Alex had been so unhappy here when he was a child.

'What if *we* live in it? The location's perfect—it's only an hour out of London by train. We can keep the flat for when we're working late and make this our home.'

'But…you don't want this, do you?' Marie looked around the large sitting room. She could almost see their children playing here. 'The decor…'

'The decor can be changed. You could make this into a wonderful room. We could keep the piano.'

That would be nice…

'And there would be loads of space here to set up an office. We could convert the west wing and run the main charity from here.'

This place could be a wonderful family home. The kind Alex had always wanted and Marie had always dreamed of.

'What do you say to this? We'll bring some of our things down and camp out here for a while.

It'll give us time to go through everything, and then you can decide how you feel about living here.'

He wrapped his arms around her, holding her close. 'That would be perfect. Where do you want to camp first?'

'The summer house?'

They should start with the place he liked the best. Alex had written about the summer house as the one place where he had been able to get away from the stifling hold of his family.

He chuckled. 'That sounds wonderful. I'll wake up and make love to you in the morning sunshine.'

'How do you feel about a trial run now?' Marie smiled up at him. 'The afternoon sunshine might do just as well?'

He grabbed the richly upholstered cushions from an ugly sofa, loading half of them into her arms.

'I'll race you there...'

EPILOGUE

The first weekend in February

FOR THE FIRST time in twelve years the plan had changed. Only half the group had arrived at Alex and Marie's home on Friday afternoon; the rest were due the following day. They'd spent a relaxed evening around a roaring fire in the sitting room, celebrating the eve of a wedding.

In the morning Alex had walked to the old church in the village, surrounded by family and friends and with Marie's mother on his arm. After Zack had left home to go to art college she'd moved to be near her other son in Sunderland, and she loved village life there and the cottage Alex had bought for her.

He sat nervously in the front pew, waiting for Marie. 'Have you got the ring, Zack?'

Marie's three brothers had fought over who was to give her away, and in the end her two elder brothers had been given the task, and would both accompany her up the aisle. Alex had claimed Zack as his best man.

'No.'

'What?'

'You've already asked me a hundred times. I thought I'd try a different answer and see how that went.' Zack patted the pocket of his morning suit. 'I've got the ring.'

'Don't do that to me, Zack.' Alex tried to frown, but today wasn't the day for it. 'You're supposed to be a calming influence, not frightening me to death.'

Zack's laughing reply was lost in the swelling sound of the organ as it struck up the 'Wedding March'. Alex turned and saw Marie and his heart leapt into his throat. He was marrying the most beautiful woman in the world.

Her dress was the simplest part of her attire, the soft lines complementing the riot of flowers in her bouquet. The Amour de Coeur hung at her throat, its sparkle dimmed by her smile.

'You're sure about this?' Zack leaned over, whispering in his ear. 'You've still got time to run...'

'Be quiet, Zack. Of course I'm sure.'

The day had been wonderful—one delight after another: the warmth of family and friends, the way Marie had looked at him as they said their vows... Marie was the most precious thing in his life, and he knew she felt the same about him.

Their reception had taken place back at the home Alex had thought he would never return to, which Marie had made into the place he loved most in the world. Zack had come up with a surprisingly short but touching speech, blushing wildly as he'd sat down to a round of hearty applause.

'I'm so happy, Alex. I love you so much.' Marie whispered in his ear now, as they danced together.

'I love you too.'

That was all he needed to say. It made everything complete. His life and hers were woven together now, and it was a bond that couldn't be broken.

He led her over to the table where their ten oldest friends were sitting with their families. Hugs and kisses were exchanged, and Sunita whispered in Marie's ear.

She laughed, her fingers moving to the Amour de Coeur. 'Yes, it's real.'

Sunita's eyes widened, and Will laughed. 'It's your own fault, Sunita. If you *will* insist on marrying a farmer and burying yourself in the countryside, then you're going to miss some of the gossip. Don't you read the papers? We're in the presence of royalty.'

'You're joking! I *knew* I should have come last

night and not this morning. Which one of you is it?'

Alex chuckled. 'Well, technically speaking, it's both of us now. But actually I'm just Marie's loyal and faithful servant.'

'Stop it.' Marie's elbow found his ribs. 'Let's drink a toast, and then Alex will tell the story.'

There were two toasts—the usual one *to us all*, and one to the bride and groom. Then Marie sat down next to him.

'Start at the beginning.'

He rolled his eyes. 'Again?'

The story had already been told more than once.

'That's okay. I'll hear it again.'

Will settled himself in his chair and Alex realised that everyone around the table was looking at him.

Marie took his hand, squeezing it. This was no longer his story, it was theirs, and he loved it more each day. They'd rewritten it as a tale of hope—one which would endure in the bricks and mortar of the clinics they planned to build and run, and in the family they'd raise here.

'A hundred and ten years ago...'

* * * * *